THE CATACLYSM

The entire world seemed to be ripping apart at the seams and toppling off its axis. The final, cataclysmic Day of Judgment had arrived.

Into this utter chaos came thousands of locusts, flying about the tomb in a clicking, buzzing frenzy. The two men and the witch used their fists to beat the swirling black mass of insects away from their faces. And through the terrible clamor of locusts, violent earth tremors, and their own shouts and curses came the blood-curdling baying of wolves and mad dogs.

Then, in a flash, the whirling tumult disappeared as suddenly as it had started. The locusts were gone. The earth was once more inert. The winds had vanished. And the tomb was as still as universal death. The only disquieting change, which each of them felt, was the presence of some new awesome force.

"Look!" the witch screamed in exultation. "Xusia lives!"

Cromwell and Malcolm rushed to her side and gazed into the casket, grimacing with revulsion and astonishment at the sight.

The slab of red marble was gone. In its place was a pool of blood inside the casket. In the midst of this crimson broth stretched a long, thin, leathery-skinned creature whose bulbous head, closed lids, utterly hairless face and head, scrawny body and distended stomach made him resemble a jaundiced but newborn human—but one that was already fully grown and whose parents might have been ghouls. On his parched and pleated face were stamped the telltale signs of centuries of depravity and evil.

"The sorcerer!" Cromwell exclaimed.

"May we not live to regret this day!" Malcolm muttered, jumping back from the casket as if touched by fire.

THE SWORD AND THE SORCERER

by Norman Winski

based on the original screenplay by

Tom Karnowski, John Stuckmeyer and Albert Pyun

PINNACLE BOOKS   NEW YORK

THE SWORD AND THE SORCERER

Copyright © 1982 by BLC Services, Inc.

An original Pinnacle Books edition, published for the first time anywhere.

First printing, March 1982

ISBN: 0-523-41787-X

Printed in the United States of America

PINNACLE BOOKS, INC.
1430 Broadway
New York, New York 10018

THE
SWORD
AND THE
SORCERER

One

IT WAS AN UNHOLY AND HOWLING NIGHT, fit for neither the ancient gods nor ordinary men.

With each jagged burst of lightning across the rain-lashed heavens the enraged hydra-headed beast the sea had become seemed that much closer to crushing and devouring tiny Tomb Island. The coastal waters encircling this rocky site boiled and erupted with mountainous waves—the pounding and ripping claws of an advancing typhoon.

This barren strip of land was called Tomb Island because of its sepulchral rock formations and tomblike caves, and because the commoners, serfs, and shepherds on the mainland believed that the souls of demons, witches, wizards, and murderers resided there. The handful of mainlanders who were foolish enough to investigate whether this belief was pure myth or grounded in reality never returned.

Neither gods nor ordinary men would have dreamed of plowing through the violent upheavals of the sea on such a night and to such a fearful place. Yet even now a single, storm-battered galleon dropped anchor in a sheltered cove off Tomb Island.

But Titus Cromwell, the fierce warrior-king of Aragon who commanded the galleon in question, was far from being an ordinary man. The wake of his many years as a campaigning general was strewn with hundreds of men he had personally dispatched to eternity with his dreadful sword. In his heart seethed enough hate to propel him through several typhoons, while his mind burned with the single-purposed vision of usurping the richest kingdom of the known world—Eh-Dan.

It was the energizing combination of his monumental hatred and obsessive vision that had enabled Cromwell to brave the storm and now steel himself for an even more malevolent undertaking. Whereas the typhoon represented pitting his wits and mariner's skills against natural elements, the immediate and dire challenge that awaited him on the island defied the natural, rendering his prowess as a soldier and cunning as a leader useless in the face of the supernatural.

For these reasons, Cromwell brought to Tomb Island, in addition to two of his top aides and a cadre of his best warriors, the wizened, loathsome old crone chained in the hull of the galleon. Without her black arts he had no chance of welding the universally dreaded Xusia to his cause— Xusia, who, because of his consummate evil, had lain for many years imprisoned by the powers that be in a deathlike trance.

Sheltered from the rain by an overhanging cliff, four cloaked figures stood impatiently watching the six soldiers in chain mail break through the outside cavern wall with picks and shovels. One of the figures was Cromwell. The heavy rains abetted the soldiers' efforts by loosening the rocks and earth. Breaking into the tomb this way was vastly superior to attempting to clear the huge boulders that sealed the mouth of the cavern. That would have taken a whole battalion of Cromwell's men.

"Faster, you dogs!" Cromwell barked at the diggers. "Or you too will end entombed on this vile pile of rocks!"

The soldiers redoubled their labors, for they had seen too many bloody results of Cromwell's hellish wrath.

Each of the four figures held a torch and the dancing tongues of fire cast an eerie glow on their faces, which were beaded with rain and sweat.

Cromwell's darting black eyes, set in features that seemed chiseled in cold stone, were reptilian in their coiled intensity. Nor was there any mistaking the creases of ruthless ambition on either side of his wide red rip of a mouth. Implacable resolve coupled with insatiable lust for power were qualities permanently etched into his fierce yet noble face.

The slouched, battle-weary figure closest to Cromwell was General Malcolm. Torchlight cruelly underscored the ravages of drink and drugs on his gaunt, strained face.

Directly behind the King of Aragon fidgeted Cromwell's minister of finance, pudgy and effeminate Lord Buckingham. As usual in the face of any danger Buckingham was scared as a rabbit trapped in a cave. And although Cromwell found Buckingham's cowardice and propensity for heavy perfumes and young boys distasteful, he tolerated his peccadillos. No one had a better head than Buckingham for inventing reasons for levying taxes on the rabble or for thinking up new ways of enriching Cromwell's coffers with gold and talents.

The small, shriveled figure hunched in front of the king was that of Ban-Urlu, the aged but powerful witch he had had his soldiers pluck from her lair in the forest. Her hawkish face by torchlight was even more repulsive to behold than during the day. With long hairs shooting out of a large black mole on her knobby chin, stark white eyeballs surrounding blazing green orbs, and sunken cheeks, Ban-Urlu resembled a nightmare incarnate. Nor did the stench of her unwashed body and the residue of odors from years of living in dank, fetid forests lessen the revolting sight.

The howls and roars of the raging storm persisted as the soldiers' shovels and picks continued to scrape and break rock. Suddenly a huge slab of stony earth and rock caved inward and Cromwell had his opening into the cavernous tomb.

"Follow me, oh mighty king!" Ban-Urlu excitedly shrieked, plunging into the womb of blackness inside.

Though the witch had never been on Tomb Island before, some dark sixth sense unerringly led her through the twisting tunnel. And as she scurried ahead of the three wary noblemen like a rat hurrying to where it knew there was food, Ban-Urlu's beaky face and crooked frame grew increasingly animated with the fervor of adoration. For to Ban-Urlu the creature they sought in the tomb deserved adoration and worship. In the realm of witchcraft and sorcery to which she be-

4

longed, Ban-Urlu was a mere practitioner while Xusia was a demonic god.

The flaming torches in their hands cast long, moving shadows of the four figures on the sweating walls. None of the savagery of the night was heard inside the mountain. Except for the sound of their own breathing and their uncertain feet the silence was total. Yet it was an evil, pregnant silence, out of which the intruders intuitively knew some kind of horror could be born at any minute.

As they walked stoop-shouldered to avoid hitting their helmeted heads against the low-ceilinged tunnel, an unearthly glow began to blossom at the end of the long passage.

Ban-Urlu started salivating at the sight of the soft, reddish illumination.

Cromwell's right hand gripped the bejeweled hilt of his well-honed sword; whatever threat that strange glow at the end of the tunnel denoted, he was prepared to grapple with it.

Malcolm rubbed his bloodshot eyes and wondered if that unholy light was not the product of the wine and opium he had imbibed the night before.

Lord Buckingham had never seen such a sinister-looking shine before. He began to tremble and glance longingly over his shoulder toward the makeshift hole through which they had come.

"Sire, would you deem it disrespectful if I waited for you outside?" Lord Buckingham asked meekly.

"Make one move to leave us," Cromwell growled, "and your dubious balls will dangle from the tip of my sword!"

The ruby-red glow grew brighter the closer

they got to it. Suddenly they found themselves passing the threshold of a cavernous chamber of rock, where they saw, awe-struck, the source of the supernatural light.

In the center of the deathly still tomb was a massive casket made of some material Cromwell had never seen before. Lodged in the top of the casket was slab of red marble, gleaming like the huge red eye of a dragon. It was from this mysterious stone that the unwavering stream of almost mystical light poured.

Cromwell and his men guardedly moved toward the magnificent coffin, but Ban-Urlu motioned that they stand back. Her protruding eyes feverish with anticipation, the twisted witch raised one of her emaciated hands and pointed to the luminous casket.

"It is there that our prince of demons sleeps!"

She kept inching closer and closer to the casket until she hovered adoringly over it, herself bathed in the unearthly illumination. Slowly, with the controlled sensuousity of a young woman caressing her lover's back, the old hag began to lustfully stroke the glowing stone, her withered face afire with some secret rapture. And as her hands lovingly caressed the marble her normally raspy voice made soft cooing, purring noises.

Cromwell studied the old crone with disgust. Spittle dribbled out of the corners of her caved-in mouth and the dilated pupils of her green eyes tilted upward into her sockets. For a fleeting moment the witch reminded him of the look of ecstasy on the wench who rode astride him the night before. He shuddered. To imagine that old bag of bones in a sexual context was enough to make him want to retch!

6

"That's not a man's shaft you stroke, you filthy old hag, but a casket! Get on with it!"

Ban-Urlu hissed and threw him a jaundiced look. But she instantly stopped pawing the stone and wiped the contempt from her face when she saw Cromwell's menacing scowl. The murderous king's volcanic temper was known and feared throughout Aragon. And to end her life impaled on his sword before the casket of Xusia would damn her soul to drift through space for eternity!

Without a word, Ban-Urlu untied the lizard-skin bag from the rope about her waist and removed a small, ornate oil lamp. Using her torch to light it, she set the urn on the marble stone. An eerie finger of mind-altering smoke rose from the lamp and she drew the smoke deeply into her lungs. Now Ban-Urlu began to shuffle and whirl around the casket, bowing obsequiously in the direction of the coffin. As she worked herself into a state of possession Ban-Urlu uttered the same incantation over and over again:

"Xathos makid asom bacathulu, macathulus!"

It was the arcane language of another age, long, long ago. The longer she chanted the incantation the plainer it became that she was in communion with invisible spirits. Perspiration broke out on her face, while the modulations of her voice suggested several other voices speaking through her. Once again Ban-Urlu's green eyes rolled upward into her sockets, leaving only the whites exposed. Over and over she droned,

"Xathos makid asom bacathulu, macathulus!"

Now as she circled the casket for the tenth time she began to shudder and stagger, knocking up against the glowing coffin, acting as if occult

7

forces were using her as a channel to enter the precious thing lying inside the casket.

Buckingham was trembling uncontrollably and glancing incessantly over his shoulder, as if fixing to flee. When his gaze returned to the hag, who was reeling like an old drunken whore, and he saw what was happening to the casket, the torch slipped from his hand to the ground and he had to steady himself against the moist wall to keep from keeling over.

The same sight evoked a different response from Cromwell and Malcolm. They unsheathed their swords and assumed a defensive position. But even while they did these things they knew their weapons were powerless against the metamorphosis taking place before their incredulous eyes.

In a matter of seconds the three men witnessed the casket become composed of hundreds of tortured human heads, some of them actually moving.

Next the tomb began to hiss and swell, with a demonic chorus whispering the same incantation coming from Ban-Urlu's bloodless lips.

Suddenly an icy, foul wind exploded into the tomb chamber. Cromwell and Malcolm automatically hoisted their swords and exchanged glances of disbelief when they realized the terrible wind emanated not from the outside but from somewhere within the casket.

The wind rapidly became a fierce gale causing their long cloaks to flap, while whipping up the tomb's ancient dust in great, choking clouds. Only Ban-Urlu seemed impervious to the dreadful tempest, as her voice and the sibilant whispers of demons blended with the typhoonlike wind. Cromwell, Malcolm, and Buckingham could hardly remain upright as the tempest knocked them about. They had to bury their faces under their cloaks to escape being blinded and suffocated by the churning dust and great veils of cobwebs.

Gripped by stark terror, Buckingham was beside himself. His short pudgy arms flayed at the buffeting wind as if warding off invisible attackers. He was absolutely convinced that if he didn't get away from this horrible place he would perish. Bending his head as far as his inflated stomach, he bucked and charged through the wind toward the tunnel with every ounce of strength he possessed, teary pleas for help issuing from his blubberous lips.

Buckingham's piercing cries jolted Ban-Urlu out of her trance. When she saw he was trying to leave the tomb she screamed at him.

"Stop, you fool! On your life do not leave this chamber!"

Whether from the shock of Ban-Urlu's screeching warning or from the lashing wind, his short, stubby legs lost balance and he fell on his helmeted head, the impact of the hard ground on metal instantly plumeting him into oblivion.

Suddenly the ground beneath them began to shimmer and shake. What felt like a tidal wave hitting the tiny island deflected their interest in Buckingham's fate to their own safety. The next second the unmistakable rumbles and seismic concussions of an earthquake tossed the stunned trio to the floor of the tomb, rocking and shaking them as if they were in the palsied hand of a giant. The whole world seemed to be ripping apart at the seams and toppling off its axis. The final, cataclysmic Day of Judgment appeared to have arrived.

Into this utter chaos materialized thousands of locusts, flying about the tomb in a clicking, buzzing frenzy. The two men and the witch used their fists to beat the swirling blackness of insects away from their faces. And through the terrible clamor of locusts, violent earth-tremors, and their own shouts and curses came the blood-curdling baying of wolves and mad dogs.

Then, in a flash, the whirling tumult disappeared as suddenly as it had started. The locusts were gone. The earth was once more inert. The winds had vanished. And the tomb once again was still as universal death.

The only disquieting change, and which each of them felt, was the presence of some new awesome force.

Slowly the trio scrambled to their feet, their eyes focusing on the now steaming casket. Cromwell gestured that Ban-Urlu should approach it first.

The screwed-up features of her hag's face once more alive with adoring anticipation, Ban-Urlu staggered to the casket and peered into its now open interior. Immediately she grew incoherent, her face moving in uncontrollable contortions.

"Look!" the witch screamed in exultation. "Xusia lives!"

Cromwell and Malcolm rushed to her side and also gazed into the casket, grimacing with revulsion and astonishment at the sight that confronted them.

The slab of red marble was gone. In its place was a pool of blood inside the casket. In the midst of this crimson broth stretched a long, thin, leathery-skinned creature whose bulbous head, closed lids, utterly hairless face and head, scrawny body and distended stomach made him resemble a jaundiced but newborn human—but one that was already fully grown and whose parents might have been ghouls. On his parched and pleated face was stamped the telltale signs of centuries of depravity and evil.

"The sorcerer!" Cromwell exclaimed, recoiling a few feet when Xusia's hooded eyes sprung open.

"May we not live to regret this day!" Malcolm muttered under his breath, also jumping back from the casket as if touched by fire.

Like a slimy serpent rising from the marshes to survey the approach of enemies, Xusia slowly rose out of the casket to a sitting position, blood dripping from his triangulated features, while his huge reptilian orbs quickly adjusted to conscious life again. When his transfixing stare rested on Cromwell and Malcolm, for them it was like gazing into a blazing infinity of unregenerate sin. And when the sorcerer opened his thin-lipped mouth, the foulness of his breath bore the smell of decaying corpses.

Now those same malevolent eyes shifted to Ban-Urlu, who was close to the casket gleefully cackling and triumphantly rubbing her hands over the resurrection her magic had wrought.

"Who art thou, hag?" Xusia's voice seemed to drag up from the bowels of his being, raspy, deep, resonating throughout the tomb.

Dazzled by the honor of being addressed by this ancient and most powerful of demons, Ban-Urlu fell to her bony knees and prostrated herself before him. But when she spoke in her whinning manner, her voice betrayed cold fear along with joy. For she knew that the blood-drenched sorcerer could snuff out her life with but a wish. And

11

the chilling thought swept through her that perhaps Xusia, after a thousand years of uninterrupted sleep, might resent having been awakened.

"Oh great, dark Lord . . . I am called Ban-Urlu. A witch of the Sani Order!"

Though his arms were spidery thin and his body wasted, superhuman power nevertheless streamed from some inner wellspring of his being. And it was felt by all three intruders. So palpable was Xusia's powerful presence that when he addressed Ban-Urlu again, for her it was like once more being pushed backwards by the force that had raged in the tomb only minutes ago.

"I thank thee for the work done in my behalf. Rise!"

The sorcerer held out his blood-smeared hand to the thrilled witch. In appreciation of his gesture Ban-Urlu reverently took his extended hand and proceeded to lick and suck the blood from Xusia's fingers.

"Disgusting pig," Cromwell grumbled, removing the helmet to brush his blond, matted hair from his forehead.

The remark now drew the hideously grinning sorcerer's attention to him.

"Careful, sir!" Malcolm whispered. "The thing did not like your comment."

"And who might thou be?" Xusia sized up every well-hewn part of Cromwell's sinewy body.

The king decided that it was time they stopped being so awed by the loathsome creature. Xusia might misinterpret awe for weakness. The moment to assert his sovereign authority over the sorcerer was now.

Cromwell's hand once more resting on the jewel-encrusted sword, he pulled himself to his full height and majestically declared, "I am Titus Cromwell! Supreme King and Lord of Aragon!"

Xusia smirked. "Your underling and the hag are properly humbled by me. Yet you show neither respect nor fear. Pray tell me why?"

"I have slain dragons far greater in strength than yours, Xusia. Besides, I know the mystical law decrees you must serve the man who brings about your resurrection . . . or you risk eternal damnation."

"Ah. Now I understand. Ban-Urlu has initiated you into some of the secrets of our Black Bible. Very well. What is it you wish of me?"

"I need your help in conquering Eh-Dan. It is the richest kingdom in the civilized world, and I must have it! You will help me achieve that dream."

While Cromwell and Xusia conversed, Malcolm and Ban-Urlu listened and watched enthralled. If the two most ruthless and powerful beings on earth should join forces, the pact could affect the destiny of the world for centuries to come.

"But you still have not adequately explained why you need my services. You are a king, with a network of spies and one of the most powerful armies on earth."

"Yes. And I have conquered many kingdoms, but Eh-Dan has always escaped me. Four times have I been defeated by the indomitable King Richard of Eh-Dan. But with your aid and my army, I know this time I will be victorious!"

"And if I still refuse?"

"Either you assist me or I will unleash all my forces to destroy you."

"And if I should comply, what reward wouldst thou bestow upon me?"

13

Malcolm swallowed his fear, pushed the hag aside and stepped forward. "The life we have given you, toad, should suffice! Besides, what assurance do we have that your reputed powers aren't based on pure superstition?"

Xusia glared at Malcolm and hissed. How dare this insolent, dissipated swine question his mantric powers. He would show the scum, all of them, what his unearthly powers could do, right here in the tomb, now! Then he would see them cower and display the respect that he deserved!

Xusia's hooded slits shifted from the two men to the witch.

Discerning the spite and fury on the sorcerer's face, Ban-Urlu began to tremble.

"Of thee," Xusia hissed, "I have no further need!"

"Aaaahhh!" she screamed, realizing she was about to be sacrificed to entertain the cruel king and debauched general. "Please, master, no! You are my dark lord—my god! It was my incantation and magic that made life's juices again flow in—Aaaahhh!"

Her frail body jerked and lifted several feet off the floor, dropping on the ground like a sack of flour.

Cromwell and Malcolm backed against the wall to watch Xusia's grotesque display of wizardry in action.

The sorcerer raised his bloody, taloned hand toward the witch and opened his palm, as if to release an unseen missile into her body, galvanizing her off the floor to her feet again. Excruciating cries of pain flew from her as she twisted, writhed, and tossed about the tomb in a paroxysm of agony. Cromwell and Malcolm nearly retched

14

before the sight of the green bile and smelly urine erupting from her mouth.

Throughout the witch's agony Xusia rocked in the casket with demonic laughter. Now the sorcerer raised both arms and aimed them at Ban-Urlu. Whatever kind of malevolent force shot out from those thin, scaled arms hit their target, for the witch clutched her titless chest and the cracking of bones and ripping of flesh resounded throughout the chamber.

Their strong backs still pressing against the walls, with grim fascination the two warriors watched Ban-Urlu's still beating heart tear from her mashed and shredded chest and fly through the air into Xusia's outstretched hand—still pumping and squirting blood.

Cackling madly, the sorcerer stared at the dead witch's heart and petted it, as if it were a prize bird he had caught.

Sick to death of Xusia's gloating demonstration of power, Cromwell rushed to the casket and, before the sorcerer realized what was happening, the King pressed the edge of his gleaming sword along Xusia's throat. "Enough of this nonsense!" Cromwell bellowed. "You've made your point!"

Xusia dropped the heart beside the gory body of the hag and grinned at Cromwell, pretending he was oblivious to the blade at his throat. "As you can see, my art is powerful!"

"Do we then even need my army?" Cromwell baited him.

"Even sorcery hath need of swords and the warriors to wield them."

"Then you will do as I ask?"

Xusia nodded.

Cromwell withdrew his sword and inserted it

15

back into its sheath at his side. "I will let you live, sorcerer, so long as you serve me well. But betray me," the King warned, his brow knitting with menace, "and I will joyfully send your spirit back to rot for another thousand years!"

Xusia's face lit with a demonic radiance. "Thou shall have thy kingdom and I, too, shall have what should be mine."

Cromwell stood back to watch Xusia slither rather than climb out of the casket, gore oozing in rivulets down the sorcerer's emaciated, malformed frame.

Had he made an irreparable and terrible mistake in resurrecting Xusia? Or did the event mark an alliance that would carry him to the kingship of Eh-Dan—and tomorrow the world?

Two

IT WAS A SEA-MOIST, bright spring morning and Elysium, the capital of Eh-Dan, shimmered with radiant light as if encapsuled in a giant glass bubble.

Built around a natural half-moon bay, for many centuries this bustling and prosperous city had been the cultural and commercial center of the ancient world. Because of the medley of nations that sent precious wares for trade to Elysium—sensuous houris from Persia, salt and wines from decadent Rome, silver and diamonds from Zimbambee, myrrh and spices from Egypt—the city was a melting-pot of races and influences from East and West.

Elysium was a veritable treasure chest of riches, a prize that many foreign kingdoms had tried in vain to wrest from its benign but invincible monarch—King Richard, who ruled over his contented subjects from a castle on the highest summit overlooking Elysium and the azure sea beyond.

The castle was made of rough-hewn gray stone

17

and was surrounded by beautiful gardens, with a maze of paths, islands of riotously bright flowers, gleaming pools, and magnificent statuary. The labyrinthine interior had as many resplendent chambers as it did hidden tunnels and dungeons known to the king and a precious few alone.

On this particular late morning, the entire city was astir with the spirit of celebration. For it was the much beloved king's sixtieth birthday. A colorful pageant of events was planned: puppet shows, tumblers, jesters, singers, actors, tournaments and jousts of sundry sorts. In appreciation of this radiant outpouring of love from his people, Richard had ordered his emissaries to bestow upon every man, woman, and child of his kingdom a gold coin.

A special celebration feast for the lords and ladies of the King's court awaited Richard's arrival in the main banquet room just outside the garden.

But while the festivities were already in full swing throughout Eh-Dan and the castle, a less than celebrant King Richard stood on the garden terrace waiting for his lovely queen to join him.

On the surface Richard pondered the majesty of the capital stretched out below him, glittering in the sunlight like a cache of jewels. But inwardly he brooded, sorely disturbed by the recurrent nightmares he had been having before his soothsayer's death. That was a week ago. The dreams were all filled with terrible portents involving sorcery, betrayal, and the dismemberment of his loved ones. Amilius had been on the verge of deciphering the nightmares when he suddenly died, the victim of a mysterious disease.

Richard's dark musings were interrupted by the

18

appearance of two of his children, five-year-old Natalia and Talon, his precociously serious and warlike fourteen-year-old son. Richard wiped the worry off his face and held outstretched arms to both children. But gay Natalia ran into them first and he lifted his saucy and only daughter high over his head, kissing her on the way up.

"We're all waiting, Papa! Your birthday feast is ready!"

"I'll be along shortly, my treasure! Why don't you and Talon go first and make sure everything is properly ready."

Natalia smacked her lips with anticipation. "Does that mean I get to taste the cake—to see if it's good enough for you to eat?"

Richard chuckled, for a while forgetting about the nightmares and rumors of Cromwell amassing another army against him.

"Of course, my angel! You're my royal taster!"

He lowered Natalia to her feet and she instantly sprinted from the terrace in the direction of the feast, her mind filled with visions of the enormous white cake she had seen earlier.

When he turned to Talon and saw the frown on his already manly face a pang shot through his heart. The boy's gloomy disposition of late made Richard wonder if Talon had somehow discovered, perhaps through court gossip, that he was not the legitimate son of the king and queen but was, in reality, the bastard offspring of a night Richard had had with a harem wench—a beautiful and intelligent damsel but a lascivious wench nevertheless. And was the stain on Talon's birth the reason why he had always favored the boy over his older son, Duncan?

Richard kissed Talon on the cheek and sadly

19

studied Talon's brown cloak, brown cowl, and brown puffed-sleeved tunic. "You dress too somberly for one so young, my boy. And why that dark cloud on your comely brow?"

Talon accepted his father's mild reproof unflinchingly. "Why is it, Father, that Duncan will get to go on your expedition and not I?"

Richard was somewhat relieved. Behind the frown was the boy's frustrated eagerness for battle, not what he had thought.

"Next year it will be your turn. Your older brother is all I can handle this time." The truth was he didn't want Talon's superior swordsmanship to outshine his older brother's just yet.

Talon shrugged his shoulders and shuffled inside, stopping in his tracks about ten feet away. Without turning around Talon defiantly asserted over his shoulders, "I can whip Duncan blindfolded."

"I know, son. Unfortunately—so does he."

Talon nodded and dejectedly left his father standing outside the chamber on the expansive terrace.

With his strong-willed son gone, Richard returned to dissecting his nightmares, searching for meanings behind the cryptic symbols in them. But no sooner did he get started then he heard the rustle of the queen's robes behind him.

He spun around and saw Malia sauntering toward him with tantalizing hints of her bountiful body through tight misty-blue-gray robes. He smiled, pleased with the sight of her. Her hair the color of tarnished gold, her skin smooth and pink as an infant's. Malia at midpoint in her life was more arousing to him today than when he first bedded her, when she was but fifteen and he was already a man. He had never put much value on virgins anyway. Did not everyone know that a lute gave off sweeter music the more it was played?

Richard's wet lips brushed her cheeks and she flushed. His hair and short, neat beard might be white but beneath his dark tunic she knew Richard was as lean and hard as the night she first felt the thrust of his formidable shaft.

"Why do you tarry out here on the terrace, dear husband? Everyone awaits you at the feast." She tried to sound as gentle with him as possible. He had not been himself since Amilius' death.

"I've been obsessed with those infernal dreams, dear wife. They still haunt me."

"Was Amilius able to give you any enlightenment about them before he died?"

He started to reply that of one thing the soothsayer had been certain; the nightmares boded evil tidings for the kingdom of Eh-Dan. But he thought better of it. Already worried as she was about Talon's moping about the castle, this was not the time to add to her cares. He tried to adopt a happier mien.

"Amilius did say that a king rules better when he plays harder!"

The queen knew the game he was playing. He was trying to spare her feelings.

"That doesn't sound like the Amilius I knew."

Richard locked his arms about Malia's waist and drew her to him. Peals of merriment from the feast drifted to where they stood. "I'm tired of the routine, my love. Tired and bored. I long to set a stallion between my legs and be off into the horizon of adventure!"

"You're too old for that sort of thing. Besides, you are the king and kings have duties."

"A pox on duties, I say!" The warm sun and the

21

press of her body against his own started to kindle his passions and he kissed her on the mouth, slipping his tongue between her moist lips.

Breathless but enjoying his upsurge of virility nevertheless, she gently but firmly pushed him away.

"What has come over you, husband! You're acting like a child—a wanton one at that."

Aware of the dent in her self-control his enflamed kiss had delivered, Richard smiled and refused to be put off.

"Duncan is old enough to watch the throne in my absence. Let's not tell a soul and go off by ourselves for a spell—like two young lovers stealing away for a tryst!"

"Darling, there are hundreds of people waiting for us at the celebration in your honor! We can't just bolt off on impulse like common people. You're the king and I am the queen!"

"Which is precisely why we can get away with doing things others cannot!" He embraced her again. "Grab only what you need, woman, and we're gone for a week, or two—or a month if you like!"

Malia giggled like a girl, warming to the idea of a spur of the moment holiday. Then she saw her brood of children walking along a garden path toward them and the girl within instantly became the responsible mother and queen again.

She disengaged herself from Richard's arms. "Careful, husband. The children are here."

Accompanying Talon and Natalia were Duncan and Henry. Duncan was eighteen and rapier-thin like his father. Henry was ten and blonde and sleek like his mother. With the exception of

Talon's drab garb all the children were dressed in their gayest finery.

"I'm hungry, Father and Mother!" Natalia whined. "And so is everyone else at the feast!"

Richard and Malia exchanged looks of dutiful resignation, held hands and proceeded to lead their brood along a rose-flanked path to the waxing din of revelers drinking and laughing.

As they approached the brightly bannered and festooned archway to the feast area they nearly bumped into Phelan, the royal appointee to the throne, who was also hurrying late to the celebration. Sprightly trailing after their father was Phelan's young daughter and only son, Alana and Mikah. The boy was as sturdy for his age, fifteen, as his sister was lyrically beautiful and mature for her thirteen years.

"Whoa, Phelan!" Richard jokingly chided his closest and most respected advisor. "There's enough food for you, your charming fledglings, and everybody else in Eh-Dan on this day!"

Phelan laughed, adjusting the silver belt girding his paunchy stomach, which not even his long white tunic could conceal. "We both appear to be running behind, beloved sovereign. But I must place some of the blame where it belongs." He fixed Alana with a mock stare of annoyance. "My beautiful daughter is much worse than her mother used to be. She'd doll up till donkeys learn to whistle if you'd let her!"

The two families laughed while Alana blushed and acted as if she weren't aware of Talon's bold examination of her person.

Richard recognized the all too familiar fire in Talon's dark eyes and smiled. There was more than lust for battle burning in his young loins.

And no one but an eunuch would argue that Phelan's girl was desirable. She was only thirteen but already ripening curves and the upward tilt of virginal breasts were temptingly outlined by her clinging gown. But for Richard Alana's most arresting feature were her smoldering dark eyes, which already held the promise of fleshy pleasures and the self-conscious knowledge that beauty was power. If Talon was a man in a young boy's body Alana was a woman in the body of a girl.

"I'd say she was definitely worth waiting for," Richard teased both Talon and Alana. "Would not you, Talon?"

But the two blossoming striplings were now so engrossed in each other that they didn't realize the king was addressing them.

"I *said*," Richard repeated, louder, "Alana is worth waiting for ... eh, Talon?"

This time the smitten pair had heard and while Alana modestly turned her inviting gaze away from Talon, he continued unabashedly to stare at her.

"Ay, father. She is indeed."

Richard and Phelan laughed.

"Oh, to be young again, eh, Richard!"

"The sleepless nights! The hammering desires!"

"Oh, leave the children alone!" the queen playfully reproached her husband and friend, while shooing her delighted brood in the direction of the festive clamor.

Talon strutted alongside Duncan, Henry and Mikah, while Alana held hands with the queen and Natalia. The king and Phelan headed the party, chattering about court politics.

Approaching the gaily decorated archway, with

glimpses inside of boisterous revelers around a huge banquet table and pretty maids carrying trays ladden with food, Richard suddenly stopped his royal entourage. For General Karak was racing toward them along another garden path, waving his arms for them to wait.

When Karak caught up with them he was breathless and his normally stern face seemed sterner.

"What is it, General Karak?"

"Forgive me, sire. But I have just received important news from our army on the eastern front."

The queen automatically shepherded the children away from the three men. From experience she knew Richard did not like to discuss military matters in the presence of her and the children. This consideration was another reason she loved him so much.

Richard indicated that Malia was to wait while he and Phelan conferred with Karak. He steered the two men even farther away to make sure the queen and the children were out of earshot.

"Now, General Karak, tell me precisely what has happened."

The general's immobile features seldom conveyed little more than a dour sternness toward life, a trait that often bothered Richard because he could never be quite certain what Karak was really feeling or thinking. But this time the corners of Karak's stretched mouth and shaggy reddish eyebrows escalated up and down. Clearly the tidings he bore were of great import.

"Sire, reports are that a huge mercenary force, led by Cromwell of Aragon, has invaded the eastern border."

The news was like an ax to his head, splitting

him in two. Cromwell. His old enemy. The nightmare was coming true. Pray God not all of it did!

"Cromwell, you say? So the rumors were true."

Karak nodded.

Phelan rested an arm around the king's shoulders. "Just like the monster to attack on your birthday."

Another macabre scene from the nightmare slid into Richard's mind and he hesitated asking the next question, but finally did.

"Is . . . is there any word of black sorcery with Cromwell's assaults?"

Phelan and Karak looked at Richard, puzzled. It was well known that the king prided himself on being rational and that he put little stock in sorcery.

"No, sire. None. Why do you ask?"

"It's not important. Can the border army deal with Cromwell's forces?"

"Without a doubt, sire. The eastern army is one hundred thousand strong. And Mogullen leads them."

Richard's sagging spirits lifted. Mogullen was one of his bravest and most skillful generals. "Good. But send couriers to Rinak and Lambona. Tell them to ride to Mogullen with reinforcements. And keep me posted daily of the turn of events."

Karak nodded and scurried away to carry out the king's instructions.

Richard observed Phelan suspiciously marking Karak's departure.

"You've never trusted Karak, have you?"

Phelan nodded.

"Yet he has never given the court any cause to doubt him."

"A man's face that I cannot read—ever—worries me."

Richard affectionately slapped Phelan on the back and pointed him toward the waiting queen and their children. "We have too many concrete reasons to be concerned without harboring imaginary ones. Hush now, and say nothing to the queen about all this."

When they rejoined Malia she neither hinted nor pried into the nature of Karak's business. Besides, if there was trouble in the kingdom, in deference to her feelings, Richard would not tell her anyway, until it was absolutely necessary.

With Richard, the queen, and Phelan at the head of the party, the two families resumed marching toward the feast.

Just outside the archway of the banquet room, Richard suddenly halted the party and pulled back. The queen searched deep into her husband's lean face.

"What troubles you, Richard?"

Richard glanced down the garden path over which Karak had swiftly faded away, seized with sudden dread. If one part of those hideous nightmares has already come true, perhaps the rest of them would too. Instead of participating in a celebration he should be at General Mogullen's side grappling with Cromwell.

"You know how inept I am, good woman, at hosting these affairs arranged in my honor." He rested a hand on Phelan's shoulder. "Let our beloved friend here attend in my place."

The queen smiled. Sixty. A king. And he was still shy. So that was why he was behaving so peculiarly!

27

"Richard, my love, it is *your* birthday party, not Phelan's!"

"The queen's right, Richard. The peerage in there anxiously waits to demonstrate their love for you, not me. It would be neither civil nor politically wise to disappoint them."

Before the king could protest, the queen grabbed him by the arm and practically tugged him toward the increasingly louder revelry. Except for Talon, the rest of the children couldn't suppress laughing at the sight of the king being pulled by the queen like a stubborn mule on a rope. Only Talon correctly surmised that his father's faltering had more to do with Karak's tidings than facing an unruly crowd of well-wishers.

As the royal party marched through the garlanded and bannered archway a roar of cheers and birthday greetings exploded at the sight of the king and his retinue of loved ones.

In the midst of this jollity and display of love Talon's and Alana's eyes locked, sending messages of intimacies to come. On impulse Alana sidled up to him and kissed him wetly on the cheek, then darted to her father's side before Talon could react. When he recovered from her boldness, the predatory set of his features relaxed and he looked like any ordinary teenage boy who realized he had just fallen in love.

Three

SHORT AND ROCKLIKE IN BUILD, General
Mogullen gropingly opened the flap of his tent
and peered outside into the night. He was weak,
bewildered, and mortally sick—as were most of his
men—with a mysterious plague that was a
hundred times more deadly than Cromwell's
lances, swords, and crossbows. Underneath
Mogullen's sectional helmet—consisting of a visor
and a headpiece—he could feel running sores
opening up like malignant flowers on his scalp
and the back of his muscled neck, while life's vi-
tality slowly ebbed from him as if he were being
bled.

He was getting so feeble that he had difficulty
focusing. Then the blur cleared and he could discern the sea of tents covering a plateau above a
river bank. Bonfires flared here and there like
flaming roses, the light silhouetting bodies strewn
about the demolished camp like smashed flies. His
nose had no difficulty identifying the stench of
men recently butchered by the knives of war.

Mogullen lifted his unshaven, swollen face toward the heavens. A galaxy of stars hung over the eastern front of Elysium like glittering daggers waiting for a signal from God to drop—drop and mercifully put out of their misery the legions of his men who lay wounded and dying out there, felled not by the military might of Cromwell's puny five to eight thousand soldiers against his 100,000 men, but by an unseen specter, a specter that had all the earmarks of having been wrought by black sorcery.

In all of Mogullen's thirty turbulent, carnage-filled years as a soldier he had never witnessed the hideous likes of what had happened on the field of battle here today!

Because Cromwell's attackers were so prodigiously outnumbered and poorly equipped, Mogullen's army had been swaggeringly cocky about the outcome of the unfolding siege.

"We'll have Cromwell's parts for you by sunset," one of his best lieutenants had boasted.

Considering the staggering odds in their favor the boast had not seemed an idle one. On the contrary, as Cromwell's men advanced upon their impregnable line it looked like a suicide attack if there ever was one. Mogullen had all the advantages: superior numbers, experience, more weapons, and the vantage point of being above Cromwell's men as the horsemen and foot soldiers marched toward Mogullen's camp.

Then the unbelievable horror occurred, like a hellish blast from the underworld.

When Cromwell's army was within striking distance, Mogullen gave the order for his archers to release their rain of arrows. But as the missiles sprang into the air, an invisible hand seemed to catch them in flight, causing the arrows to go awry and fall ineffectually to the ground. Simultaneously Mogullen's men began to moan, retch, and double up, suddenly racked with excruciating pain.

In the grip of this mass and crippling seizure it was child's play for Cromwell's army to storm through the defense line and proceed to hack and cut and devastate Mogullen's army. Sawing through the ranks like a horde of farmers cutting down wheat with scythes, it took Cromwell's soldiers less than an hour to turn Mogullen's camp into a wasteland of bodies.

Nevertheless, because of Mogullen's greater numbers and the renowned valor of his soldiers, they were somehow able to repel the attackers. But even now, as the wobbly general stared despairingly out over the night-cloaked and body-laden battlefield, he could hear in the distance Cromwell's army boisterously preparing to strike again—and this time there was no hope of repelling his troops a second time.

Aware that the cursed plague was ravaging his body so fast that he would be mercifully spared having to see the final death-blow to his army, Mogullen staggered back inside the tent. He grabbed the edge of the map table to support himself.

He was standing this way when the young rider he had sent for burst into the tent, his own breastplate and beard caked with blood and dirt. The sores erupting on his battle-weary face showed that he too was afflicted with the plague but he was not as far gone as Mogullen or the others.

At the sight of his beloved general's condition

31

tears came into the rider's eyes and he used both arms to steady him.

Mogullen mustered what little strength he had left to speak.

"Ah, Robert, you come at last! You must ride immediately to Elysium! Tell the king himself that our men are dying by the thousands. A plague has been thrust upon us. The battle is lost!"

Mogullen desperately gripped the young rider's collar, the light beginning to leave his eyes.

"Tell King Richard . . . tell him that it is black sorcery we fight, you hear—black sorcery! The hope of all rests with his learning this. Black sorcery. Now go!"

Mogullen's lids clamped shut and the rider knew he had given up the ghost. Collapsing in his arms, Robert gently laid to rest the general's body on a fur-lined cloak in a corner of the tent, weeping copious tears.

"God take thy soul, General Mogullen," he whispered, dashing out of the tent to his waiting steed.

He knew he would have to ride faster than he ever had in his entire life, for he could almost hear the flapping wings of death hovering over him too.

Four

BRIGHTLY LIT WITH TORCHES that burned
night and day, Richard's massive, high-vaulted
war room was on the ground level of the castle
and loaded with trophies from previous cam-
paigns: a suit of armor from Eric, the terrible king
of Woodlands, whom Richard had beheaded with
one fell swoop of his sword; a velvet tapestry
whose golden thread depicted Richard's victorious battle against the barbarians from the east;
and a multitude of other souvenirs from different
engagements.

It was here that Richard plotted war strategies
with his staff of royal generals and where, surrounded by symbols of triumph, he liked to come
whenever he felt insecure, deriving some renewal
of self-confidence from these glorious reminders of
former conquests.

And it was here that Richard came directly
from the celebration several hours ago, hoping to
clear his head of the effects of too much mead and

to slay the fear that the rest of his nightmares would also come to pass.

Richard stood by the light of the tall cathedral window, through which he could see out into the courtyard and observe the two guards posted there, as he affectionately polished his awesome tri-bladed sword; each blade was spring-loaded and the weapon served the dual purpose of three swords in one and flying missiles when desired. He had personally designed the weapon and the most famous swordmaster in Eh-Dan had forged it for him. Because of the myriad of enemies the tri-bladed sword had vanquished it was his most cherished possession.

An unholy chill went through Richard at the sound of a galloping steed in the cobblestoned courtyard, followed by the harsh cries of his guards. "Who goes there? Halt if you value your life!"

"My God!" Richard said aloud to himself. Was not this also a piece from his nightmare!

"Sheath your swords!" Richard heard the rider shout in a failing, pain-racked voice. "I have a message for the king from General Mogullen! I must . . ."

"Catch him—he falls!" one of the guards yelled.

"Bring him in," Richard shouted through the stained-glass window, his voice resounding in the vast war room.

Richard bolted to the outer chamber as Phelan and one of the guards half-dragged and half-carried the young rider to the king. Richard knelt and looked aghast at the lesions and pus-oozing sores on the messenger's face. He did not need to be a physician to perceive that the soldier would soon die.

"Get him a leech!" Richard instructed the guard and then gazed at Phelan for answers.

"He will speak to no one but you," Phelan explained, also kneeling beside the dying messenger.

Richard snaked an arm under the messenger's back and tilted him forward, compassion and anger mingling in the gesture.

"What is your report, son?"

Fever and creeping death made the rider's eyeballs swivel, trying to find the king's face.

"Sire . . . the eastern army has been . . . been destroyed!"

An invisible spear went through Richard's heart. He now knew that if he didn't act promptly all of the nightmare would soon become a reality. "Destroyed?"

"Aye, my dear king, destroyed. . . . Stranger than strange things have happened . . . a mysterious plague eats our flesh . . . General Mogullen begged me to tell you . . . just before he died in my arms . . . he begged me to tell you that it is black . . . black sor—"

The terribly lesioned soldier's head fell to one side like a rag doll's, his swiveling eyeballs now fixed for eternity. Richard gently rested the young soldier's head on the marble floor and shot to his feet, sad but aware of a rising tide of fury too.

Phelan also rose as General Karak, helmet respectfully tucked in the crook of his left arm, came charging into the war room, his stolid features glistening with sweat.

At the sight of Karak, the king exclaimed, "Good God—what next!"

"Sire! Another of Cromwell's armies is upon us! This time a full battalion of his troops have landed on the beach to the south and march toward the city fast!"

Phelan glared at Karak with unmasked disdain. "Why is it you are always the bearer of bad tidings?"

Karak responded in the language he knew best; he gripped the hilt of his sword.

"This is not the time for dissension among ourselves, Phelan," Richard chided his friend. Then to Karak he ordered, "Roust every man we have! Cromwell has to march through the Valley of Cybelle to reach the city—and we'll joust with the devil there!"

Karak bowed his head and scurried off. When Richard saw Phelan linger, obviously preparing to speak more about Karak, he motioned Phelan to follow the retreating general. "Go with him, Phelan, and see that he carries out my orders to the letter. Along the way summon the queen for me!"

Frustrated to not be able to share his feelings about Karak but aware that to force the issue would only anger Richard now, Phelan nodded and resignedly left.

"My armor!" Richard bellowed toward an archway in the war room, all the while ripping his royal robes away, boiling with revenge. Cromwell! He was the nightmare in the flesh! And if the tyrant was using sorcery—and sorcery was more than the mystical rigamarole of unthinking men—then he would test its power with his own sword!

A pretty teenage boy in black livery, with curled bangs, breezed into the war room, his rouged lips and long lashes trembling at the unusual sight of an enraged King Richard. "Yes, my lord?"

"Squire, fetch my weapons and armor! Quickly!"

The boy ran out of the room and nearly knocked into the queen, who immediately went to her husband, sorely concerned. She rested her palms on his shoulders and gazed into his grim face. "What is it, my dear heart?"

"A birthday present from the tyrant Cromwell!"

"Be more specific, Richard."

"Cromwell encroaches upon us with troops and wizardry. At this very moment his dastardly men march on the city!"

Malia pulled away and bit the back of her hand in fear. "God spare us!"

Richard took her into his arms and tried to comfort her with kisses. But she was inconsolable, knowing her husband was preparing to go into the pending fray.

"Go roust Duncan, Malia. He will ride with us. The others I leave in your charge."

"Must Duncan go too?" It was more of a plea than a question.

"Yes, my love. If he is to be king one day it is time he shows he deserves to be one."

The queen nodded, already turning to do as he bade. But she stopped just this side of the archway leading to other parts of the castle.

"You will take care of yourself and our boy!"

"You have my word on it."

She blew him a kiss and hastened away.

The king reached for the belt specially made for his tri-bladed sword, hanging on a peg on the wall, when he heard the rattle of metal behind him. He spung around and saw Talon standing before him, dressed for battle.

"The castle buzzes with news of Cromwell's army. I am ready, Father." The lust for battle glowed on Talon's face.

Richard smiled. Oh, that the boy were only a few years older and that he was not needed here at the castle more than at the imminent siege! He could use more men of Talon's courage and indomitable will.

"I'd love to have you at my side. Father and son in battle together. I've dreamed of it."

"And so I *will* be," he asserted.

"Sorry, no. You must stay behind and act as king in my absence."

Talon was beside himself with frustration. "Let Duncan be king! I want to fight, Father! Fight—beside you!"

Richard now assumed a more authoritative mien. The trick was to bridle the boy's fiery spirit without killing it.

"We each have our duties, and yours will be to stay behind and protect your mother, sister, and younger brother. The subject is closed."

For the first time in many years he saw Talon's eyes flood with tears.

"My arm is strong, Father!"

"I know it is, son, and I am proud of your prowess."

The boy's manly, comely face turned ugly with resentment. "Do you leave me behind because . . . because I am a bastard child and Duncan is not!" It was an accusation, not a question.

Guilt and remorse clutched at Richard's heart. So the boy had heard court gossip. He should have told Talon himself rather than risk his finding out the cruel way he had.

"No! And I'll hang the sow or hog who told you such a thing!" One day, if he survived Cromwell's campaign, he would confess the truth. But the

38

few moments they had left together was not the time.

He held outstretched arms to his confused and frustrated son, and Talon came rushing into them. Father and son ardently embraced, Richard covering the boy's face with kisses.

"My God, Talon, but I do love you more than life!"

"And I love you, Father!"

"Wait."

He detached himself from Talon and picked up his tri-bladed sword off the table, handing it to his son.

Talon's face was a sunburst of joy as he examined every inch of the formidable weapon. He knew how much the tri-bladed sword meant to his father, and now apparently he was giving it to him! Talon felt an outpouring of love for his father such as he had never experienced before.

"But, Father—"

"Hush. It is yours. Should I die, it will fall to you to avenge me."

For the first time Talon realized that this could very well be the last time he would see his father. And Talon wanted the king to remember him as having the courage and dignity that his father had.

"Do you understand?" Richard asked, softly.

Talon nodded and refused to shed another tear. "Yes. I understand."

Talon laid aside the tri-bladed sword and grabbed hold of Richard's forearm in the salute of the gladiators. Father and son smiled and beamed love to one another.

Five

DAWN OOZED OVER THE BLACK HORIZON like a bleeding wound. Oh how cruelly fitting an image! Richard mused, looking away from the reddish glow to the carnage all around him.

Heavy with grief and woe, Richard trudged through the Valley of Cybelle like a drunken man, stumbling and shuffling in futile search of some drop of comfort for his aching despair. A handful of his knights in full battle dress walked wearily behind him, the same hopelessness and abysmal despair on their faces.

Richard's eyes were bloodshot and puffy from unrestrained sobbing. For over a quarter of an hour he wandered through the gory chaos, gazing dumbstruck at the mangled bodies, the ulcerated faces, shorn and torn limbs, the steaming guts of dead horses, the flowing blood, columns of smoke and the broken swords and lances. He cursed Fate for not allowing him to arrive in time to die a noble death with these brave men and gallant loved ones. Death would have been infinitely sweeter than the bitter cup of reality he now had to drink.

Over there lay Phelan, his beloved friend, his face frozen forever in the agony of a plunged sword. Goodbye, sweet sage!

Dangling by the neck on a rope from a tree was Knight Edward, his dear cousin, his tongue protruding from his mouth and his gouged eyes now slits of red jelly.

And lying in a puddle of his own blood was Richard's beloved son, Duncan, his face twisted in pain from the ugly sword sticking out of his youthful chest. Oh, the heart-rending sobs that would tear from the tender bosom of the queen when she learned of this tragedy!

And in the midst of Cromwell's barbarous spoils vultures began their hideous vigil of waiting for rotting flesh to become their food.

As if a bucket of icy water had been thrown in Richard's face, he suddenly shuddered and in an instant threw off the paralysis of grief, riding an upsurge of scalding hate. He jerked his flashing sword into view and began brandishing it wildly over his head. The knights watched, transfixed to the spot, mesmerized by the king's sudden burst of fury and strength.

"I want Cromwell's head! Bring me Cromwell so I can drink his blood!"

Like a man far younger than his sixty years, Richard began to run furiously, his knights following, in the direction of the campfires on a cliff overlooking the Valley of Cybelle, where he knew Cromwell's troops were entrenched—and no doubt swinishly celebrating their victory.

"Give me Cromwell's blood, I say!" he kept yelling. "I want Cromwell's blood!"

* * *

Cromwell kept massaging his right biceps under the iron mesh shirt. His sword arm was sore. He must have lopped off a dozen heads and twice as many limbs in the lightning-quick annihilation of Richard's army. His battle dress looked like a butcher's apron, splashed with gore as well as sweat and dirt.

Cromwell was standing on the cliff's edge beside Malcolm and General Quade, the three of them victoriously surveying the havoc his forces and Xusia's sorcery had wreaked upon the Valley of Cybelle. The devastated camp below was bathed in hot morning light and there wasn't a stir among the tens of thousands of ravaged soldiers strewn there.

Cromwell was smirking. After he had made so many unsuccessful incursions into Richard's rich kingdom, the jewel of the western world was finally his!

"Over a hundred thousand warriors killed in a single battle! Incredible!"

The gruff exclamation came from General Quade. And the savage glee on his rough-hewn features was that of a man who would rather spill blood than make love.

"Aye," Malcolm concurred, pausing to swig a mouthful of wine from the goatskin flask he had pulled from his saddle. "Xusia is mighty indeed."

"I think perhaps *too* mighty," Cromwell replied ominously. "We have awakened a sleeping tiger . . . and who knows when a tiger will decide to devour its keeper?"

"When do we destroy him?" Malcolm asked, shuddering at the prospect of having to face the disquieting presence of the sorcerer again.

"I ordered him brought here but a while ago."

General Quade was disturbed. Destroy Xusia? Perhaps the most powerful weapon a general could ever hope to have? "We're going to kill the sorcerer now? But what of future battles with Richard's soldiers?"

Cromwell looked impatiently at Quade. "There will be no more battles. Richard is finished. We have destroyed his army."

Quade was still reluctant to lose the sorcerer. As an ally Xusia was invaluable. "But the commoners are fiercely loyal to Richard! They will rally to his aid!"

"Stop opposing me, Quade! We can deal with the rabble without the aid of an unpredictable wizard. And now is the ideal time to be rid of him. He is weak from the exercise of magic he has performed today. When I saw him last he looked like a vampire bat perishing from lack of blood."

"Our king is right, Quade. If we wait and his powers are restored, we might never be rid of him, and he might use his sorcery against us."

The sound of clanging chains, breastplates, swinging swords and mail distracted them. When they turned toward their tied steeds, they saw ten of Cromwell's Black Klaw warriors approaching, pushing a man in leg irons and shackles in front of them. Cromwell instantly recognized the prisoner to be Richard. Not even the swelling bruises and smears of blood on his face could conceal those noble but detested features. Cromwell puffed up and flushed with the heat of victory.

"Richard! What a surprise!"

The mockery in his voice amused Quade and

43

Malcolm while lifting Richard's drooping head defiantly.

The Klaws tossed the captured king at Cromwell's feet.

"How did you manage this?" Cromwell ecstatically addressed the Klaws.

The senior officer stepped forward, pointing to Richard. "He and a handful of knights were trying to free our prisoners. We killed the knights when they resisted and thought we had better bring the king to you, sire."

Cromwell beamed approval. "And well you did. Now leave us."

The Klaws walked away, heading for the sea of tents behind them.

Cromwell now stared disdainfully at the bedraggled and defeated king, who lay in a heap before his feet. "A king risking his neck for his lowly scum," he jeered. "How noble!"

Richard glared at his tormentor. If only he had his sword and was alone with the tyrant! "If you mean to kill me, devil, do it now and be done with it!"

Cromwell crouched beside Richard and looked close into his face. Daggers gleamed in the eyes of both men. "Order your subjects to lay down their arms," Cromwell baited, "and proclaim me king! Do that, Richard, and you and your family go free!"

Before Cromwell realized what Richard was about, the shackled king took aim and spat into Cromwell's face.

"Dog!" Cromwell bellowed, wiping the mess off his chin and lashing the back of his hand across Richard's face.

The slap stung terribly but it was worth it to

see Richard humiliated before his men. "Free my hands, you son of a dog-faced jackal, and I'll varnish the ground with your brains!"

Still on his knees, his face inches away from Richard's, Cromwell dropped all pretense at civility and sneered. "At this moment, Richard, my agents are preparing to murder your family! Only by your agreeing to what I say can save them! The right words from you and—"

Before Cromwell finished the sentence, Richard lunged at him and wrestled him to the ground.

"You tyrant! You scum! You—" He stopped reaching for Cromwell's throat at the flash of a dagger in Quade's hand.

"Die, Richard!"

"Not yet!" Cromwell screamed.

But Quade's four inches of blade was already plunging through Richard's throat with the ease of a knife going through butter.

Richard toppled off Cromwell's chest and fell to the ground, a fountain of blood gushing from his neck.

Cromwell jumped to his feet and violently shook Quade. "Jackass! You killed him too soon! I had plans for him!"

"Cromwell—look!"

It was Malcolm, tilting his chin in the direction of Xusia, who dragged his bent figure towards them. Cromwell released Quade's shoulders, used one booted foot to roll the lifeless body of Richard over the edge of the cliff, and faced the exhausted sorcerer.

In his voluminous black robes and cowl Xusia's wasted form seemed lost. And the sluggish movements of his whole being reaffirmed how debilitating his work in Cromwell's behalf had been.

Even the gleaming intensity of his reptilian eyes had faded, leaving opaque orbs, swiveling laboriously.

Cromwell vibrated with grisly excitement. The time to scotch the snake was when he was weak, not when he was in full striking force.

"Thou hast sent for me?"

Xusia's voice was funereal, hoarse, in keeping with his deathlike appearance.

"Behold our hero!" Cromwell mocked.

"Get to the point, king! I'm weary from labors in your behalf!"

Swiftly and stealthily was the way to catapult this half-human, half-ghoulish creature into eternity. Using his cloak to conceal the action, Cromwell deftly unsheathed his dagger and held it hidden at his side.

"Weary you are, sorcerer? Then you should rest—forever!"

Bemused and befogged with tiredness, Xusia did not see the knife but felt it ripping open his belly. "Oh treachery most foul!" he shrieked, reeling backwards as he tried to clamp the eruption of blood with both hands over the wound. Before he could cry out again the scoundrel Quade drew his sword and sliced him across the back and chest. Dizziness blinded him but he felt the cruel shove and kick from someone and a darkness darker than the darkest night enveloped him as he careened headlong over the cliff.

Cromwell, Quade and Malcolm stood watching Xusia soar downward until he hit the ground, hundreds of feet below. Surely every bone in his body must have been broken upon impact.

Cromwell looked over his shoulder at the fading Klaws. "Several of you fetch the sorcerer's body below!"

The cadre of soldiers heard his booming command and immediately started running down a twisting path that led to the bottom of the cliff.

"Well, that's that," Quade said, sorry to have lost so potent a weapon as Xusia.

"Not quite," Cromwell hissed, pushing the general also over the cliff. Quade's trailing scream sounded like a falling meteorite.

"He was a coarse man," said Malcolm.

"His breath always bothered me," Cromwell quipped. "But his willfulness and covetous looks at my crown bothered me even more."

The Klaws who had been ordered to recover Xusia's smashed body used the vulture hovering in the sky as a beacon to where the sorcerer lay.

"We should have brought a shovel and bag," one of the soldiers remarked. "Surely after that fall the sorcerer will be more mush than solid."

"Look!" Another Klaw pointed to the vulture they had been following and who was now flying away from the site where they estimated Xusia lay. "First time I ever saw one of those scavengers fly away from a waiting dinner."

When the Klaws arrived at the spot where they expected to see the repulsive remains of Xusia they froze in their tracks.

The sorcerer was gone.

In the clean white sand was a bloody outline of where a man had recently lain—but there was no sign of Xusia anywhere. Nor were there any footprints to indicate that someone had retrieved Xusia's body before they could.

A chill went through the soldiers as they looked

questioningly from one to the other. Finally the
senior officer articulated what was on all of their
minds.

"Black sorcery!"

Six

AT PRECISELY THE MOMENT that a knife sliced through King Richard's throat, a drawbridge at a secret castle exit fell over the moat surrounding the castle. The next moment four robed figures galloped across it into the still breaking day, headed for the green-gold cool lushness of the forest in the distance.

The moment the solemn riders touched the other side of the moat two guards rushed out of the castle to wrench the creaky drawbridge in place.

"God save the queen and her brood!" one of the guards exclaimed, watching the riders fade across the plain to the forest.

"And blessed she is to have General Karak at her side to protect her!"

For Talon a presentiment of doom seemed to thump in time with the horses' hoofs. Ever since his mother had awakened him, Natalia, and his younger brother in the middle of the night—telling them that the castle was soon to be besieged and they were to join their father—Talon sensed a danger other than the one Cromwell's troops posed. And when he discovered that Karak was leading them in this early morning flight, Talon grew more apprehensive.

Although Karak had always been respectful towards him, and he had never heard the king disparage him, there was something about Karak's cold marble features and sparseness of speech that made him feel uneasy around the general. And now this same inscrutable person was bringing them to the king. Surely his father would never entrust their lives to a man he didn't have absolute confidence in. And yet—

Talon's snorting steed vaulted a racing ford, the impact on landing jogging him back to the reality of where they were.

For several hours they had ridden hard through the forest and streams, galloping for long stretches but walking the horses through the thickets. The sunlight spilled through the leafy trees and giant foliage like a steady rainfall of gold coins. He could hear the rush of the river nearby. He knew the river and this whole forest as well as he knew the streets of Elysium. His father had taken him to hunt deer and boar here many times. If Talon had to he could spend days in the dense forest and not get lost.

"Soon, Karak?" his mother asked, her soft, silvery voice tarnished with worry.

"Ay, my queen. The river is just beyond that large grove of trees."

"I'm hungry!" Natalia whined, sitting in front of the queen in the saddle.

"Stop being a baby!" Henry chided, trying to

sound grown-up. "Soon we'll see Father and then we'll all eat."

The queen beamed love at her nine-year-old son. So tender of years and yet already so responsible and stout of heart!

Talon deliberately lagged behind the others. That way he could be sure no one from the rear could harm the queen, Natalia, or Henry. This position also enabled him to watch Karak's every move—just in case his feelings about him were correct.

The low overhanging branches and tangles of bushes forced them to thread slowly through the forest now. And the crunch of twigs and decaying leaves under the horses' hoofs sounded like popping and crackling fire. Except for these noises and the chirping of birds and the clicking of crickets, the air was charged with an electric stillness.

Suddenly they entered a clearing and there, no more than two hundred yards away, was the leap and flash of the river. Karak brought the party to a halt. The horses shook their huge heads and snorted in appreciation of the rest.

They were on a bluff overlooking the riverbank, where a small ketch was moored, guarded by what appeared to be two of the king's men.

As Karak dismounted he touched the handle of the sword hanging at his side and Talon instinctively gripped the handle of his newly acquired tri-bladed sword.

Karak approached the queen and her daughter, who were sitting astride a handsome white stallion. Without asking permission, he lifted Natalia out of the saddle and placed her on the ground.

"The king awaits you on the boat, your highness. Leave the horses with me."

He offered the queen his hand, the pasty, strained smile on his face bothering Talon more than his usually unreadable face.

Malia took Karak's hand and allowed him to help her to the ground, her long billowy robes and cape getting in the way.

"You're so kind, General," the queen said, affectionately touching his arm. She glanced in the direction of the boat. "My heart thrills at the prospect of being with the king again!"

Henry jumped out of the saddle on his own and with no small flourish of manly independence.

The queen, Henry, and Natalia walked a few yards towards the river and stopped, realizing Talon was still aloft his mighty steed, tense, expectant, battle-ready. Karak approached the young prince and offered him his hand too. Talon observed Karak's flinching jaw muscles and a twitch around his eyes. He had never seen Karak this nervous and he declined Karak's extended hand.

Karak angrily pulled his hand away. "Come now, boy—dismount!"

It was a command and nobody had ever spoken to Talon in that tone of voice save his father. Talon seemed to grow taller in the saddle as he glared down at the increasingly fitful general. "Something is wrong!"

The queen automatically hugged her children close to her. Like his father, Talon had an uncanny nose for trouble and she trusted it.

"Nonsense!" Karak flared back. "Now get to the boat!"

He reached to pull Talon out of the saddle but

he kicked him away. Karak rubbed the shoulder where the boy's booted foot had landed, peering from side to side into the surrounding forest, as if hoping no one had witnessed his humiliation.

More than ever Talon was convinced danger lurked nearby.

Karak moved menacingly toward him once more. "I said, get off that horse now, or I'll—"

With one swift jerk Talon flashed his tri-bladed sword to within inches of Karak's face, frightening the general back a few feet.

"Or you'll *what*!" Talon demanded, still brandishing the sword at him.

Panic seized the general. Without uttering another word, he tore from the clearing and began to frantically zigzag through the woods.

"Get to the boat, Mother!" Talon screamed, now certain that Karak had somehow betrayed them. "Quickly!"

Malia snatched Natalia into her arms and with Henry at her side began to run as fast as she could toward the ketch, Natalia crying fearfully.

Talon turned his steed around and took after Karak at breakneck speed. The general ran along the path they had broken with their horses.

The pounding of the hoofs and the driving obsession to get Karak at any price for the moment eclipsed Talon's concern about his mother, baby sister, and brother. "Treachery must be punished with the sword," he remembered his father once saying, and Talon welcomed being Karak's executioner.

"Father! Father!" Henry cried for help, running to the boat well ahead of his mother and Natalia. He was only a few yards from the ketch when two hulking Klaws sprung up from lying low on deck.

They leaped to the sand and proceeded to savage the boy into bloody quarters with razor-sharp scimtars. It happened so fast that Henry didn't even have time to scream—but his mother did, for the whole grisly slaughter happened before her and Natalia's eyes.

Now Natalia's screams fused with her mothers, but Talon heard none of it. He was too engrossed in bearing down on Karak.

The general was running out of breath and he knew he'd certainly never outrun Talon's stallion so he decided to stop running and fight the enraged boy.

But no sooner did Karak unsheath his gleaming sword and whirl around to take his stand against the prince than Talon galloped along side him and severed his head with one swoop of the tribladed sword, sending it rolling into the bushes. Karak's body stood headless for a moment before falling to the forest floor.

Talon reined his horse to a halt. His lean, hard body pulsated with the excitement of his very first human kill. With Karak now dead, his mind instantly snapped back to the fate of his family. He hoped to God they were all safe with his father on the boat!

He turned his steed around and began galloping back toward the beach.

But Talon didn't get beyond the clearing when two Klaws jumped from behind the trees not ten yards in front of him and aimed crossbow pistols at him. Talon's quicksilver reflexes came to his rescue. With the first sign of movement from the trees, Talon yanked on the reins and the horse reared high on its hind legs. The action lifted Talon above the oncoming arrows but exposed his horse's barreled flanks to them. The horse shrieked with pain as the metal-tipped arrows ripped through bone and entrails. As the horse crashed to the ground it tossed Talon out of the saddle. But even as he was flung through the air he held on tightly to his tri-bladed sword. And when he landed he somersaulted to his feet, ready to grapple with the attackers. But no sooner was he upright when the two Klaws fired their crossbow pistols again. Talon dodged one arrow but the second one pierced his left hand, the impact slamming him against a tree, where his hand was pinned by the arrow to the tree. "Ohhhhh God!" he groaned and wailed with pain, but still clutching his sword with right hand. Every time he tried to wrench his hand from the tree he nearly passed out from the excruciating pain.

Since Talon was seemingly helpless, and not knowing the capabilities of the strange-looking sword in his hand, the Klaws smugly took their time reloading the crossbows.

"Did you ever see a prettier boy—or an easier target?" one of them taunted.

They both laughed, giving Talon the chance to aim his tri-bladed sword before they could fire. He pressed the release latch and fired one spring-loaded blade and then the other—both blades hitting their marks in the chests of the soldiers. It happened so unexpectedly that both Klaws fell dead on the ground before they knew they had been pierced.

The sight of their twisted features and shattered chests in no way alleviated Talon's own pain—nor the horror that was unfolding before his eyes on the beach. Even at this distance he could perceive his mother and Natalia despairing over

55

the prostrate body of his younger brother. "Oh, Father, where are you!" he grievously screamed, once more vainly trying to dislodge his bleeding hand from the tree.

Out of the forest's edge by the beach, Talon saw at least a dozen Klaws emerge and, swords drawn, slowly encircle his mother and sister.

"No! No!" he agonizedly shouted, knowing that, even if they could hear him, his supplications would not dissolve those metal hearts. In another second the closing wall of Klaws totally hid the queen and Natalia from view. But when he saw the Klaws raise their flashing swords and begin to chop and thrust, he knew exactly what was happening to his mother and baby sister. For a few moments Talon went insane with frustration and rage, and he pulled wildly, frenziedly on freeing his hand, this time indifferent to the pain. But it still wouldn't budge.

Then a brutish Klaw broke loose from the circle of soldiers, carrying his screaming and kicking sister. She had been spared the swords for an even more heinous fate. Once again Talon tugged and wrenched at his riveted hand, bellowing with pain and helplessness. *You'll pay for this, Cromwell—I swear by Almighty God you will!*

From a tree-sheltered perch on a bluff overlooking the river, Cromwell and Malcolm had been able to observe the massacre of the queen and the youngest boy, as well as see the abduction of the little girl. Cromwell smiled lewdly.

As for the fiery colt who had taken after that bungling fool Karak—he couldn't possibly have slipped alive through the net of Klaws he had deployed throughout the forest. Like his father and the rest of Richard's cursed family, the boy called Talon also had to be dead, his body either bristling with arrows or hacked to pieces by swords.

"Come," Cromwell gestured to Malcolm, who looked badly in need of a drink. "I want to see for myself if the queen's breasts are as lovely as rumor says they are!"

Malcolm nodded and obediently followed his king, but wished he didn't have to. His stomach was still queasy from vomiting a full liter of wine and he was afraid that the sight of all that gore would make him retch once more.

The mutilation of the queen proved to be even too much for Cromwell. He and Malcolm were now on their way into the forest to ascertain the fate of Talon.

But when they arrived at the site where the boy should have been, instead of his savaged remains, nothing of him was in sight. In his place were two of Cromwell's crack archers, their chests ripped open, with no sign of the sword or the terrible weapon that did the job.

From triumphant cockiness Cromwell's mood changed to instant rage.

"Find the bastard boy!" he shouted to the Klaws who were emerging from their hiding places in the trees. "Find him or your lives are worth nothing! He has to be nearby! I want him!"

Malcolm noticed a broken arrow drenched in blood sticking out of a tree. He suppressed calling Cromwell's attention to it. Anyone who distracted Cromwell from one of his tirades invariably became the object of that rage.

Red beads of blood dripped through the branches to the foot of the tree. Talon prayed that the Klaw walking directly under him did not see the blood, praying also that he could continue to throttle the scream of pain that was trying to escape from his throat. The loss of blood had left him only half conscious. His left hand was a mangled mass of raw meat with a jagged puncture through the middle of it. To stanch the flow of blood he had torn off his outer tunic, wrapped it around his hand and pressed the bundle between his thighs, closing them together. Later, when it was safe to come down from the tree—if he did not bleed to death first—he would staunch the wound with a compress of the dead horse's dung and sodden leaves, as his father had taught him to do. And if he survived . . . he would devote . . . devote the rest of . . . of his life to avenging his . . . his—

The rest of consciousness drained suddenly out of him like water running into sand. He collapsed into the arms of a huge branch out of sight of anyone moving below.

Seven

THE HUGE YOUNG MAN wore a dark gray woolen cloak and the chain mail of a warrior. The gusty breezes on the high bluff overlooking Elysium blew his shoulder-length, raven-black hair behind him. His eyes were bluer than the sky above him and were flecked with fierce pinpoints of gold. His dark, finely chiseled features and muscular form beneath his garb resembled the statue of Apollo his father had once brought back from a campaign in Hellas, and he knew it. The young man was aware that most women found him desirable and that men praised his statuesque figure.

Yet there was precious little conceit in Talon's personality. He had been taught by Malia—long before the wandering mercenaries found him half-dead in the forest and nursed him back to health—that a man's self-worth should come from performing noble deeds, not from the accident of comeliness and wealth.

If Talon had any conceit about his appearance

at all it centered around not his Apollonian face and form but, ironically, a slight deformity. That deformity being the steel brace covering two of his fingers and a portion of his left hand, wrapping around his wrist like a gauntlet. For that once agonizingly maimed hand had become a proud symbol of his will and ability to survive. In addition this minor impediment had spurred him to work ten times harder than most warriors to become proficient at handling all kinds of weaponry.

The steel claw was also a constant reminder that he had a score to settle with Cromwell, face to face. No matter how many conquests he continued to make, on the battlefield and in bed, Talon would never live easy in his own skin until Cromwell was impaled on his three-bladed sword.

Talon continued contemplating the city of Elysium sprawled below him, waves of sadness going through him. It was more than eleven long, battle-weary years since he last saw the once dazzling and happy capital of Eh-Dan. As a boy he had stolen to this very site countless times to gaze enchanted at the seaport city's splendor and bustling activity. But what a change! Whereas ivory turrets, bejeweled spires and gold domes once sparkled in the sun, the precious stones and metals had been stripped away, leaving bare wood and stone. Whereas Elysium's colorfully dressed citizens once strode and sauntered proudly through immaculately kept streets, and vendors, strolling troubadours, puppet masters and lovers had filled the promenade along the bay, there were now more soldiers patroling the streets than citizens, and the promenade was deserted. Instead of small families going out to sea to fish and for pleasure in small brightly painted boats,

Cromwell's galleys lay at rest in the harbor like floating coffins. There was an air of neglect, poverty and oppression hanging over Elysium—a pall of misery so thick that Talon thought he could cut it with a sword.

Sadness gave way to anger and Talon spat on the earth at his feet. Cromwell's reign had turned the richest city in the western world into a cesspool of poverty and gloom.

Talon pulled his broad shoulders back, wiped away the scalding tears from his eyes and marched down the hill to join his mercenaries—a group of nine seasoned warriors from ten to twenty years older than he.

The mercenaries were weary and unkempt from weeks of hard riding and they weren't quite sure why their young leader had detoured to stop here but they obeyed him unquestioningly. He was the best all-round warrior of the lot and his judgment had proven impeccable in most instances. Besides there was an abiding love between the men and Talon. Had they not practically raised him since the day they found him writhing in pain at the foot of a tree, with that horribly mutilated hand of his? And Talon had made them proud to be mercenaries. Ever since the day they unanimously appointed him their leader they were only for hire to kings whose cause was just and noble.

With one agile bound Talon was astride his black mount.

Darius, a swarthy soldier who preferred using a spiked ball and chain in battle over the sword, turned to Talon.

"Why do we stop here, General?"

"I have a debt to pay."

"But King Lonbosha awaits us in Malodon."

"He can wait."

Determination was like steel in his eyes.

Ishmael, whose lust for sensual pleasures was a standing joke among the men, now addressed Talon. "I think it's a good idea. I'm hungry."

Talon smiled. "For what, Ishmael—food or women?"

The mercenaries laughed.

"Both, my lord."

"We have only enough silver for one or the other." He kicked the flanks of his steed and began to trot along the road leading through the open gate into the city, his men close behind him.

"Make your choice, men," he tossed over his shoulder. "Each of us is allowed but one lust tonight!"

The closer they rode to the city the more grisly signs of Cromwell's tyranny they saw.

Off the road to their left was a partially burned down thatch cottage with a wooden sign on a stake in the scorched earth, reading DEATH TO ANYONE WHO MALIGNS CROMWELL'S NAME!

A little later an emaciated boy of ten years or so, dressed in rags, ran out of the bushes and tried to keep pace with Talon's slowly moving horse. "Please, sire! Food or a coin for food—please!"

Grim, Talon tossed the boy several silver coins and pressed on. His men had never seen him in such a solemn and dangerous frame of mind.

As they wound round a bend in the road they heard a strange, creaking noise. Seconds later they saw the macabre source of the creaking. A peasant and what looked like his son dangled from a rope tied to a tree, their necks broken, their faces frozen forever in contortions of pain. At the foot of the tree were the hideously mutilated carcasses of what must be the wife and daughter of the man swinging from the tree.

Afraid that if he lingered before this repulsive sight he might show more emotion than he wished to in front of his men, Talon galloped forward, slowing down when he heard his men thundering after him.

"I heard this is the way things go in Elysium these days," Ishmael dourly remarked when he caught up with him.

Darius, riding on the other side of him, asked, "Did you ever see Elysium in its prime, Talon?"

"Yes," Talon gloomily replied.

"Was it a happy place?"

"Oh yes!"

In remembering happier times, for a fleeting moment the fierce warrior looked like a little boy.

Moving furtively out of the sunlight into the thick shadows of a waterfront street was another grim young man—not as large and handsome as Talon, perhaps, but every bit as fearless and thirsty for Cromwell's blood.

Though he tried to hide his identity in the voluminous folds of his cloak and cowl, he had no way of knowing that his identity was already known to the six soldiers who stealthily trailed him, no more than a dozen or so stone abodes away. Although the sun gleamed like a shield of gold in the sky, the light bouncing off of it washed one side of the street and left the side where the soldiers stalked their young quarry full of inky shadows.

The dark-featured young man rounded a corner away from the harbor and stepped into a smelly alley, between a grain depot and a closed blacksmith's shop. A tall, slender and even darker man, also in heavy robes, detached himself from the shadows and detained him.

"All is set, Mikah," he whispered, gazing into the feverish brown eyes of the young man, which were so much like his father's, Phelan.

"Excellent, Machelli! Excellent!" Mikah glowed with excitement. At last the opportunity to cut down his father's killer had arrived!

Machelli rested a hand on one of Mikah's shoulders. "By this time tomorrow you will be sitting on the throne of Eh-Dan—its legitimate heir."

Mikah could feel strength and cunning beaming from Machelli. He was so grateful to have him on his side and not Cromwell's. "The people of Eh-Dan owe you everything."

Machelli shrugged his shoulders and tried to make light of his role in the overthrow. "Justice is its own reward, Mikah."

Now the intense young man affectionately grabbed one of Machelli's sturdy arms. "You're a good man, Count Machelli."

The count looked toward the brightly lit mouth of the alley. "But it is dangerous for us to tarry. You and I can have no further contact until after the deposing of the king."

Mikah released his arm and nodded. "So be it. I will see you then, dear friend, when Eh-Dan is free!"

"Yes—when Eh-Dan is free!"

With those last words, Machelli slipped out of the alley before Mikah could see the dark smirk on his face.

A few moments later Mikah was also in the street, moving in the opposite direction from Machelli. After fifteen minutes of running and walking through Elysium's maze of tiny streets and dark alleys—ducking around corners at the first sound of one of Cromwell's patrols—he stopped before a rough-hewn stone abode. Before knocking on the huge wooden door, he glanced over his shoulder to make sure no one saw him. Then he gave the secret code—two loud knocks and three soft ones.

Seconds later a portal in the door slid open, revealing two suspicious green eyes. The portal closed and the door swung inwards. Mikah slipped inside.

The rebels' headquarters was actually one vast candle-lit room, with a large wooden table and chairs at its center, around which stood four hooded leaders of the uprising. Mikah threw his hood back and greeted each of the rebels with a warm smile. He was still a trifle delirious with the good news Machelli had given him.

Now the others dropped their hoods. One of the faces that came into view belonged to his lovely sister, Alana. She had the kind of dark beauty and luminosity that illuminated any room she entered, and a vixen pout to her full lips that made men wet theirs upon first seeing them. Through a strange alchemy her countenance reflected virginal innocence side by side with gypsy passions. Mikah was sure Alana still possessed her maidenhead but the sensuous smoldering in her eyes and the liquid swing of her saucy buttocks when she walked bespoke an impatience to lose it.

"You're late," she softly chided her beloved brother. "We were worried." Her dark irises lit up like crystal as she proudly pointed to an open map on the table. "Come here, my brother, and look!"

Mikah walked to the table and with one exultant glance realized what it was.

"Uds blood! A map of the castle's secret passages! How did you get it?"

The faces of the others in the room beamed the same excitement.

Ninshu stepped forward, whose face was as craggy as his posture was straight as an arrow's. "A whore loyal to our cause pilfered it from Lord Essex himself!"

Mikah was so overjoyed that he went around the room and embraced each one. "What luck!"

Warmak, the only one of the group whose enthusiasm contained some speck of doubt, spoke up. "The lords and barons of Eh-Dan have arrived at the castle for tomorrow's royal feast. But there's something strange about the affair. The kings of the neighboring empires have also been invited to the feast. Perhaps Machelli can tell us why."

Mikah shook his head. "No. Any further communication with him is too dangerous at this date. Our people are ready. We will proceed as planned. This may be our final chance to overthrow the murderous Cromwell."

Suddenly there was a ramming crash at the door and it buckled inwards, spilling Cromwell and a half dozen Klaws into the room. Instinctively the rebels flashed their swords and stood posed for battle, though stunned into speechlessness by the surprise attack.

"Cromwell!" Mikah snarled, his sword raised chest high.

The rebels now protectively encircled Mikah and his sister.

"What have we here," Cromwell baited, "a nest of serpents?"

Out of the folds of her robe Alana pulled a dagger, brandishing it at the tyrant king. "Let's kill him now while we have him!"

Her fury made Cromwell smile. "Is that you, Alana? My, what a lovely thing you've become! What ripe fruits for me have you underneath your skirt and blouse?"

"Swine!" she screamed and lunged for him, but Mikah and Warmak restrained her, knowing she'd be dead before she got close enough to do him any harm. Now Mikah pulled her to one side and whispered in her ear, "You must warn the others! We'll cut a path for you!"

"I won't leave you!" she whispered back.

"You *must*."

Annoyed by the sister's and brother's sotto murmurings Cromwell motioned for his men to flank the rebels on all sides.

"Come, come, children—no secrets from the king. It won't do you or your rebels any good. At this moment my Klaws are dragging your dogs from their holes and putting them to the sword. Your rebellion is over."

Exploding with the rage of knowing someone had betrayed him, Mikah released a piercing war cry and the rebels began fighting their way out of the trap. In seconds the room became a whirlwind of swirling and thrusting and clashing swords, puffing and groaning men. But the rebels were outnumbered and outmatched and Cromwell's men quickly overcame the insurgents. Ninshu crashed against the table and then to the floor, a wound in his arm. Warmak fell, minus an arm, and gushed blood until he died. Walton, the gen-

67

eral who had taught Mikah everything he knew about the strategies of war, also toppled, three welling gashes over his heart.

Only Mikah was spared. And just before Cromwell knocked the sword out of his hand with one powerful blow of his scimitar, Mikah succeeded in running his sword clean through one of the hulking Klaws.

Cromwell's eyes searched the pile of bodies and shattered furniture for Alana. But she was gone. In the heat of battle she had somehow managed to escape.

"After the girl!" he yelled over his shoulder to the guards outside. Then he fixed his attention on Mikah, who stood crouched in front of him like a sleek and dangerous animal preparing to spring. For several seconds the two enemies glared at each other, panting and sweating from the fray. Mikah was acutely aware that all it took was one word from Cromwell and the Klaws would run him through ten different ways. Still he defiantly thrust his square jaw at the king. Better to die in defiance than cowardice.

Cromwell teased the gleaming point of his scimitar inches away from Mikah's ropy abdomen. "Have at me, Mikah," he goaded. "Come to me, sweet boy!"

Mikah could hold himself in check no more. He threw a wild fish at Cromwell's face but the agile king sidestepped the throw and plowed one of his own huge fists into the rebel's stomach.

Mikah doubled over and fell limply to the floor. Cromwell seized the opportunity to kick him in the ribs and guffawed triumphantly. "This is a game for men, not boys. Now tell me the name of the real leader behind the insurrection—or I'll have your nails plucked out and then your tongue!"

Cromwell kicked him once more. Just before Mikah blacked out from the pain he wondered why Cromwell thought there was someone else masterminding the revolt.

Eight

EXCEPT FOR SPLASHES OF MOONLIGHT
here and there, the night's mantle covered most of
the narrow alleys and snaky streets through which
Alana ran, breathless, the long cape covering her
blouse and skirt flowing with the wind. The rattle
of breastplates and swords told her two or more of
Cromwell's guards were closing in on her. Although her long, tapered legs were strong, she
had been running over the hilly streets for a long
time and they were sorely throbbing.

In Alana's hand she still clutched the bloodied
dagger she had planted in the guard's shoulder
who had attempted to block her escape from the
headquarters. And she would use it again and
again, even on herself, rather than be taken
prisoner. So long as Mikah lived to become right-
ful king of Eh-Dan, she would gladly die for the
cause!

Alana bolted around the corner of an unlit tavern into a long, wide, dark alley. She tried to ignore the smell of dumped garbage and urine as

70

she ran. A high wall loomed in front of her and she realized she was facing a dead end. She panicked, paused for a moment to get her bearings. She decided the only recourse open to her was to go back the way she came. Her heart thumping, her legs really aching now, she ran toward the light at the end of the alley.

Suddenly the silhouette of a Klaw materialized in that threshold of light. He began to walk in her direction. As he got close she noticed a blood-caked swatch of tunic tied around one of his shoulders. Her heart pounded like thunder. It was the guard she had stuck.

"Oh no!" she exclaimed, as the guard stalked her, his sword rattling in its sheath at his side.

"Oh yes, bitch!" he retorted, still breathing hard from the chase.

As he inched toward her she kept backing up, pointing the dagger at his chest.

The guard obscenely placed one hand over his bulging crotch. "And now I'm going to stick you with my dagger—before I slit your throat!"

The moment her back was up against the wall she lunged at him. But he ducked, grabbed her by the wrist and kept twisting it until she dropped the dagger, clattering when it hit the cobblestones. He used his burly arms to glue her curvaceous body to his and thrusting his hardness into her crotch. She vainly tried to shake herself free and to bite him but his arms were like chains binding her to him. His mouth reeked of garlic and his pungent sweat was vomitous.

"I can feel the silken purse between your legs, sweetmeat!"

He spoke huskily, brutishly.

71

"You're going to squirm on the end of my lance whether you like it or not!"

As if to seal her fate, Alana saw two more Klaws wander into the alley. They marched to within twenty feet of them and vociferously praised the tender parts of the quarry their comrade had caught. "On with the show, Rouke!" one of them yelled to the guard that held her. "But I want a piece of the pie when you're done too!" the other one exclaimed.

To the three guards' surprise, Alana suddenly stopped struggling and began to wantonly grind her lower torso up against the man called Rouke. Now her legs pumped and squirmed as if they were impatient to wrap around him. She blew hot breaths on his hairy neck and into his ear. He loosened his grip on her and pulled his head back to better study her face.

Alana smiled lasciviously up at him. "You're a *real* man," she cooed, "aren't you, pudding?"

He relaxed his hold some more, puffing up with pride in his sexual powers. "You will soon see for yourself, harlot."

"Go to it, man," one of the guards exhorted. "Can't you see she's dying for it!"

Slowly Alana worked one of her silky legs between his until she felt his throbbing manhood rest on her thigh.

He began running his coarse hands over the ripening curves of her body, her thigh against his shaft inflaming his lust.

"I'll mount you as you've never been, bitch!"

"With what!" Alana shouted into his face, at the same time ramming her knee into his genitals.

He bellowed like a bull in pain, stumbling to the wall and repeatedly hammering a clenched fist against his abdomen while he nursed his crotch with the other hand.

The other two guards rushed Alana, threw her against the wall and held her there, each man grabbing one of her arms.

Rouke swayed in front of her, still rubbing the bruised member underneath his short tunic. His face was an ugly mix of pain, anger and lust. He slapped Alana viciously across the face. She bit her lips to prevent their seeing how much the slap had hurt.

"You slut! You'll pay for hurting me!"

He grabbed hold of the blouse under her cape and ripped it open, exposing Alana's heaving breasts, which were as round and full as they were upright and rosily nippled.

The men's eyes devoured her beautiful breasts. "My mouth waters for a suck of those melons!" one of the guards moaned.

"We'll each have our fill!" Rouke shouted. "Throw her on the ground. Her time has come!"

"Nooo!" Alana screamed, preferring to die than have these coarse brutes soil her with their abominable seed.

Rouke kneeled in front of her and forced her legs wide open while the other two guards pinned her arms to the ground. She struggled frenziedly to close her legs but Rouke wedged his body between them. He threw up her long skirt, exposing her creamy flat belly and triangle of pubic hair. "Ahhhh," he growled. "The bearded rose! Let's see if there's any honey behind those pretty petals!"

Alana screamed, writhed and struggled desperately to free herself but to no avail. Her limbs were bolted to the cobbles by the three men. To

73

her horror she saw Rouke unsheath his dagger, the long blade catching sparks of moonlight. With his other hand, he unflapped the cockpiece on his tights and let spring forth his huge, savage-looking member.

Alana averted the sight of it by clamping her eyes shut, whimpering with knowledge of what was to come. Was the ultimate moment she had deliciously fantasized ever since the day she crossed the line from girl to woman going to happen on her back in a dirty, foul-smelling alley, beneath the weight of a swinish Cromwell soldier? Mercy, oh Lord! Mercy!

Rouke began stroking the inside of her thighs with the sharp edge of his dagger, reveling in the terror screwing up her pretty features. "When one dagger won't do—the other will."

He dropped the knife on the cobbles, used one hand to keep her thighs spread and with his other hand steered the purplish head of his shaft to the threshold of her womanhood.

She screamed again and again, ripping the night's silence to shreds.

"I like to hear my women scream!"

His two cohorts laughed at the girl's misery and urged Rouke to enter, so that they too could partake of her lavish body.

Just before he parted her lips with two fingers a brusque noise from behind distracted him and he looked over his shoulder.

Standing no more than ten feet behind the soldiers was a young giant of a man, smacking away on a huge bone of meat, a glitter of mischief in his startlingly blue eyes. The hand holding the thighbone was covered with some kind of a steel brace.

Rouke saw that the interruption had opened

the girl's eyes and she too stared, as they all did, at this outrageously handsome dog who dared interrupt his pleasure, only her look was fraught with shame to be seen naked and sprawled this way.

Rouke assumed he was just a wanderer off the street intrigued by the wench's screams. "Leave, pig, or die!"

The intruder didn't budge. In fact he seemed resolute to stay.

"You call *me* pig?" Talon asked with amused disdain, adding, "Sir Pig."

Rouke began to stuff his shrinking member back into his cockpiece and started to rise. "Why, you dirty rotten—"

He never finished his sentence because Talon slammed the huge thighbone he had been munching on into Rouke's face, sending him reeling unconscious to the cobbles. One of the other men went for his sword but Talon bludgeoned him unconscious too before he got off his knees. Panicky, the third guard managed to get to his feet, but in his eagerness to flee he forgot they were locked into a dead end and he ran right into the wall, head hung low, knocking himself out.

Talon roared with laughter at this bit of stupidity, even while appraising the lovely girl's face and bare breasts.

Still shaken and dazed from the ordeal, Alana started to push herself up from the cobbles but fell down again. She was weaker than she thought. The tall, broad-shouldered stranger offered her a hand and she took it. With one gentle, firm pull he lifted her to her feet but continued to clasp her hand. Energy from an inexhaustable supply seemed to pour from him through his hand and into her, reviving her.

"I owe you my life, sir."

He shrugged as if he had been doing this sort of thing all of his life and still did not let go of her hand.

"You're all right now," he reassured her. "Stop shaking. You're safe, I say."

She caught him gazing with too much appreciation at her breasts and she suddenly remembered she was naked from the waist up. She tore her hand from his clasp and covered her breasts with both hands, flushed with embarrassment.

Talon wanted to reassure her that he meant her no harm and moved to comfort her in his arms. But she recoiled and hissed at him.

"Stay away!"

He stopped and shrugged his massive shoulders once more. There was no point in remaining. She was safe now. And probably anxious to escape to some lover she lived with in one of these squalid stone hovels. He would have liked immensely to taste one of those tempting strawberries that peeked out between her fingers but that obviously wasn't meant to be. He nodded a goodbye, turned on his heels and took long strides walking out of the alley. He had more important things on his mind than wenching anyway—regardless how incredibly appetizing that particular wench happened to be.

Alana watched the gorgeous young warrior fade out of the alley, dumbfounded. Never had she beheld so comely a man. The long grey, flowing cloak he wore could not hide from her his thickly muscled body, nor the way his massive chest tapered down to slim hips. And the raw ani-

76

mal magnetism that had passed through his hand when he held her had made her nipples harden, as immodest as that might be. Surely a man who looked the way he did and who carried himself with such courtly self-assurance could not be an ordinary commoner. Even though no one was there to witness it, she blushed. Nevertheless she had been ungracious towards him. He had saved her life and instead of at least a kiss, she had given him a hiss. Should she run after him and apologize? But then he might misconstrue her intentions. What to do?

The clink and stamp of passing Klaws in an adjacent street made her decision for her. She swept her torn cloak off the cobbles, covered her nakedness, and went running after him.

When she finally reached his side he didn't drop a beat in his brisk walk, and he did not give her so much as a glance. "Wait!" she implored in hushed tones. But he kept plowing ahead. "Please, sir! I've no one else to ask for help. And you've been so kind!"

He finally stopped and gazed deep into her face. The intensity of his blue eyes sent shivers through her whole being.

"What do you want?"

"Not here . . . on the street. Cromwell's assassins are everywhere. Follow me—please! My name is Alana," she said, running ahead and assuming he would follow her.

Talon stood transfixed to the spot, trying to regain his composure, which had been shattered under the impact of what she had said. *Alana?* My God—could that sensuous feast of a girl running over the cobbles like a gazelle be *the* Alana? The erotic nymph of so many of his youthful nocturnal fantasies? Phelan's little girl and his first love? There was only one way to find out. He ran after her, his long muscular legs bringing him quickly up to her.

Nine

NO LIGHT LEAKED THROUGH the cracks in the shutters or the wooden door. To all appearances the tavern was closed for the night and the inkeeper asleep inside. But Alana knew Craccus was awake and waiting for her. By now news of the raid and her escape must have reached Craccus. And he would rightly assume she would seek refuge in his place.

As Alana used the coded knock on the tavern door she recalled that the last time she heard the code was when Mikah had used it earlier in the day, and she felt a stab of sadness.

"What's wrong?" the handsome barbarian at her side gently asked, while they waited for the innkeeper to open the door.

"Nothing."

He was puzzling in many ways. For one thing ever since he caught up with her in the street he had a look that conveyed he knew something about her that she didn't. Then there were the extremes in his behavior. He wore the rough cloak, shepherd's boots and chain mail of a barbarian. And he had the ferocity and strength to match that image, as the way he coped with her attackers demonstrated. Yet he could be gentle and he had the demeanor and aristocratic features of a nobleman. Yes, he was a puzzle.

Craccus, cagey by nature and with the features of a buzzard, opened the door and eyed the towering stranger at her side with suspicion.

"He's all right," Alana assured him.

Craccus let them in and closed the door. Before they went any further Craccus stepped in front of her, ill tidings all over his face. They were in a darkly lit hallway. Deeper into the tavern torches and candles on long wooden tables flickered in the main room. Except for two drunken rebels drinking tankards of ale at one of the tables, the room was empty. Alana noticed the young giant gazing longingly at the kegs of ale, grog and wine over a small bar.

"Cromwell's dogs have been raiding and murdering our people," Craccus spoke, his voice raspy and full of distrust. "Kalipa says your brother was captured by Cromwell himself."

Alana knew that much and was glad to hear he was at least alive. "Do you know what Cromwell intends to do with him?"

Craccus couldn't look into the girl's sweet face when he spoke again. "Alas, he plans to execute Mikah at the Royal Feast tomorrow."

"Oh God, no!"

Talon acted as if he had not heard. Better to appear detached from their cause and to remain anonymous until he knew for certain who were the villains and who were the good men in their rebellious dealings. He had already heard enough

80

to conclude that Cromwell's spies had infiltrated the rebels' ranks.

"What food have you here?"

Craccus reacted to Talon's question as if he had been slapped in the face with a fish. "You speak of food at a time like this?"

Alana scrutinized Talon's face. He couldn't be *that* callous to her feelings, not after having saved her life. She decided he was playing some kind of a game for an as yet unknown reason.

She tried to calm Craccus by kissing him on the cheek. "Pay no attention, Craccus. We must get the word out. There is to be no attack tomorrow. *No* attack. Understand?"

Craccus nodded, tossed the arrogant stranger with blazing blue eyes his most hostile visage and led them both down the hallway to a table. He shuffled away to fetch them wine.

Alana and Talon sat opposite each other on long log benches. The warm glow of an oil lamp on the table wove alternating light and shadows on their faces. But even in the dim illumination Alana could discern how sun-baked was Talon, and that his square-cut raven black hair framed his sharp features in a most enhancing manner. She guessed him to be about the same age as her brother, twenty-five or so.

Craccus reappeared and set down a flagon of wine, several drinking jacks and a bowl of dates. Talon grimaced at the fare.

"Dates! Good God, man, bring me some *beef*! I'm no bird!"

"As you wish, *sir*," Craccus said, sarcastically. "Just a leg? Or shall I bring you a whole cow?"

Talon was amused and impressed by this much smaller man's pluck. "A leg will do."

Before he left, Craccus turned conspiratorially toward Alana, ignoring Talon. "Word is being passed."

Alana nodded and watched her rescuer guzzle down a jackful of wine in one hearty gulp. He was obviously a man who enjoyed his senses and probably indulged them at every opportunity—all of them. She was intrigued by the steel brace that formed a gauntlet on his hand but didn't think it was appropriate to ask him about it now.

"You Eh-Danians know good wine," he said, smacking his perfectly carved lips.

"I didn't bring you here to get drunk."

"Why *did* you bring me here?"

"We may need your services."

"Who's we?"

"The rebels. My brother is the leader of the revolution."

"And who sits on your throne?" For the time being he thought it best to play totally ignorant of what was happening in the kingdom of Eh-Dan.

"Cromwell the Usurper. Eleven years ago he wiped out good King Richard and his whole family."

Talon acted as if he were wholly engrossed in draining the dregs of the wine, hoping to conceal the tumult the mention of his murdered father had at once stirred in him.

Craccus returned with a huge plate of still sizzling ribs and contemptuously dropped it in front of Talon and left.

Talon proceeded to attack his plate with a rapaciousness Alana had never seen in a man before. There was something almost sexual in the way he wolfed down the food. She should be thinking of her brother, period. Yet she found herself getting aroused watching his strong white teeth tear at the juicy meat, with glimpses of his long red tongue lapping the food particles from his lips. She shook her long dark hair, as if to banish these thoughts from her head. She had better get back to the business at hand.

"What brings you to Elysium?"

He flashed a wicked smile. "I haven't had a woman in weeks."

At least he was honest. "Look, I'll get to the point. I believe you to be a freebooter for hire. Am I right?"

He acted as if he hadn't heard the question, all the while boldly marking the peeks of bare shoulders her tattered cloak afforded, even as he chomped away on another rib. Sensualist that he obviously was, perhaps the quickest way to get him to talk was to appeal to his carnality.

She assumed what she hoped was her most provocative smile and sexiest voice. "I like the way you handled the Klaws back there. You're strong and quick. Is your *sword* for hire?" she asked, infusing the word with a double meaning.

His eyebrows arched and he smiled too. "Depends."

"I would pay a handsome price for it."

"If the price is right, my lady, my *sword* is yours!"

Alana rose half-way off the bench to inspect his waist and then sat down. "I don't see your sword. Do you even have one?"

He was grinning wickedly.

"Don't worry. I have one. And it is huge and made of the finest, hardest material."

"The bigger the better," she quipped, beginning to enjoy the erotic word game they were playing.

83

"What type is it, curved or straight?"

"Straight, with a very thick hilt."

"And you handle it well?"

"Very well. My strokes are straight and true."

"Oooohhh!" she exclaimed, puckering her lips. "Sounds awesome!"

"Believe me, it is. It goes deep and draws the proper cries."

Alana felt herself flush even as she uttered the next words. "I should like to see it."

Talon's blood coursed hot through his veins. "I'll show it to you in private quarters. Is there a room or a stable nearby?"

He reached across the table for her hand but she coyly pulled it away. The game was getting too serious. "Not so fast—please!"

"But my sword is poised!" he exclaimed, and to accentuate his condition he rocked the table with his knees.

The table's movements and the dire need on the handsome rogue's face made her laugh. "You are bold, sir, but nothing is free. First the task at hand."

Talon abandoned any hope of a quick tumble in the hay and settled down to the business at hand. He had been foolish to get all worked up in the first place. Surely with her brother's pending execution she had more pressing matters on her mind than a hasty joust with him. But tomorrow, or the next day, or next month, sooner than later he had to have her. No woman had ever stirred him to such depths of feeling and desire. Every fiber of his being craved to be fused with this lovely damsel. And he would never be content again until he felt her long legs wrapped around him.

"All right, then, fair lady. What do you want? A throat or two cut?"

"I want you to rescue my brother."

"And the pay?" He was still not ready to let Alana know that his interest in her brother's plight or the rebels' cause was anything but mercenary.

"Two hundred talents."

"That's not what I had in mind." He leveled his eyes at her breasts again. Even under the heavy cloak they jutted forward with her nipples clearly defined.

She pretended they were still discussing money. "All right, then—five hundred."

Let her think he was a scoundrel. He wanted her at any price. And if she did not lust for him the way he did for her, he was willing to swallow his pride and take her as payment. Either way, he had to have her. "Stop playing games," he chided. "You know what I want."

It would be too immodest at this point in their budding relationship to let him know she too ached to have their naked loins pressed together. So she feigned an attitude of great sacrifice and sighed. "All right. Anything you wish, if it will save my brother. But only one night!"

Which could just possibly lead to forever, he mused. That settled, he now geared himself for fulfilling his part of the bargain. "Where is this brother of yours?"

"In Cromwell's dungeons."

Talon shook his head, incredulous at the girl's audacity. "You want me to snatch your brother from the king's dungeons? And only for one night with *you*?" he teased. Better not to let her know he wanted her too much. Let a woman know you desired her and you gave her power greater than the mightiest of swords. "Slim bounty for such a risk, I say."

If she permitted him to get away with talking to her like that he'd think she was a whore. "You dolt!" she snarled, slapping him across the face.

Talon roared with laughter. She had fire as well as beauty. The slap only made him want her more. "All right, then! The life of your brother for one night!"

Before Alana could avert the move he reached across the table and cupped her face in his huge hands. And the gentleness she felt in them thrilled her even more than his roughness.

"I expect my bounty perfumed and prettied," he said, but tenderly.

She smiled, aware that she was looking forward to the night when she would fulfill her end of the bargain even more than he was.

Suddenly Craccus rushed to their table, killing the tender mood that had enveloped them.

"My lady! Fifty of our people have been trapped in Skull Cave by General Sades and his Red Dragon Archers!"

Alana was beside herself. "Is there any way to help them?"

"No, my lady. None. No one can save them now."

"But we can't stand by while they're butchered!"

She turned to Talon.

"How about you? Can you think of anything or do anything?" She was desperate and his cool, lofty manner in the light of this terrible development was beginning to irk her.

Over the rim of his drinking jack Talon peered

at Alana, then Craccus and then back to Alana. He couldn't be sure Craccus wasn't secretly in league with Cromwell. And for him to appear to be too willing to tackle the rebels' problems might make someone think he had a personal interest in their cause besides money. He slammed the jack down on the table, feigning anger and accidentally spilling wine on Alana's cloak. "Uds blood, woman! What do you take me for? Some mush-brained jackass?"

Surprisingly, Craccus appeared to take his side. "It would be madness to send a hundred men, my lady, let alone one."

"To risk his life is his profession!"

"*Risk*," Talon retorted, "not throw it away!"

"What's the matter, warrior," she mocked, "sword not big enough?"

He had already decided to do what he could to save the men. But he wanted to see to what lengths she was willing to go to enlist his services. "And what am I to be paid for *this* small chore?"

"I'm paying you enough for a thousand such tasks!" she snapped.

"You talk a good game, fair lady. I hope you can perform as well!" He couldn't help laughing at his own joke.

Alana tilted her pretty chin defiantly in his direction and said, "You are vulgar, sir!"

When Talon perceived her eyes moistening and he realized how much she was hurting over the trapped men, his entire demeanor softened.

"All right, Alana. I'll rescue your rebels."

Her face beamed. "And my brother too?"

"But these are impossible tasks for any one man!" Craccus cried.

"Quiet, Craccus!" She stared at the self-assured

Adonis sitting across from her, wholly confused about her feelings for him. "Well, sir?"

Next to avenging his family, suddenly giving Alana hope became the most important goal in his life. "I will retrieve both your brother and the rebels. I promise you that."

"It's suicide!" Craccus shrieked.

"Please, Craccus!"

Talon rose to his full height, walked around the table to Alana and, before she could protest, wrapped his arms about her tiny waist and lifted her off the ground. Just as unexpectedly he clamped his open mouth over hers and began to passionately kiss her. At first she tried to pull her head away but when she felt his hard tongue inside her mouth her resistance melted, and she found herself sucking on his tongue as if it were a delicious plum.

With Craccus watching, aghast by the barbarian's boldness and even more unhinged by the fair Alana's fervid responses, the kiss must have lasted a full minute. Finally the giant lowered her to her feet and released her. Embarrassed by this unprecedented display of wantonness—never in her life had she behaved this way!—she backed away from him on rubbery legs, averting his piercing blue eyes.

"I wanted a taste of your lips before being sent to my grave," he jested.

Alana lifted her head and their eyes locked. As their gazes united in intimate promises, she had the overwhelming feeling of familiarity, as if they had been lovers in an another life. He gave her another lascivious smile but it was not without tenderness and concern. Who was this irresistible enigma? A man who in so short a time had scrambled her brains and her still tremulous senses?

Before she could answer her own question, Talon strode swiftly out of the tavern into the darkness outside.

"Brash hulk," Craccus said, bringing her back to the present and the dreadful crisis the rebels were in. "Who is he, anyhow?"

"I don't know, Craccus. He never even told me his name."

"Be wary of that one, my lady. His kind is the most dangerous, for he clearly fears nothing."

What Craccus said was probably true. Yet she had perceived a tenderness and vulnerability behind the handsome mercenary's brash manner. Or was she merely seeing in him what she herself felt toward him?

"At least you won't have to worry about paying your debt," Craccus continued. "He'll not live to see the sunrise."

What he didn't know was how much she wanted to pay it. And she prayed to God Craccus' lugubrious prediction did not come to pass!

Alana suddenly remembered that underneath the cloak tightly wrapped around her she was still bare. "Craccus, can you fetch me one of your wife's robes? I will reward her later."

"Of course, my lady. Follow me."

He started to lead her toward his private quarters when the front door burst open, vomiting into the tavern a cadre of Klaws brandishing lances and swords.

"Out the back way!" Craccus shouted to Alana, as he whipped a dagger out from under his stained apron. "Run, my dear lady—and long live the cause!"

No sooner had the gesticulating innkeeper with the buzzard's face shouted his proclamation of freedom than the nearest Klaw ran his long lance clean through Craccus' puny chest, releasing a fountain of blood very much the color of the wine he served. And while four more Klaws slaughtered the two half-drunk and half-asleep rebels before they realized what had happened, another pair of soldiers grabbed Alana and carried her through the shattered door into the night, as she kicked and screamed in a hopeless effort to get free.

Ten

ABOUT THREE MILES FROM ELYSIUM'S harbor, on a lonely beach where the mountains tumbled into the sea, was Skull Cave, big enough and deep enough to house a herd of elephants. It derived its name from the peculiar configuration of boulders surrounding its entrance. As one approached Skull Cave along the beach or from the sea it resembled a grinning human skull. Because of its forbidding appearance and rumors of it being the site where demons, witches and the spirits of the dead lurked, Eh-Danians on the whole kept a respectable distance from it. But on this particular night there was more taking place at the cave than anyone had ever witnessed.

Along the beach in front of the cave were one hundred of General Sade's crack Red Dragon Archers—Cromwell's pride and joy. Their steel-tipped arrows were lodged in polished Corinthian long bows and aimed at the mouth of Skull Cave, ready to fire. Moonbeams and torchlight from the vassals nearby made the archers' hauberks, helmets and armor glitter like gold. One word from Sade, who was sitting on the backs of two girlish and scantily clad slave boys off to the side, and any of the trapped rebels inside trying to escape would be felled in a rain of arrows. And until he did give the order to fire the archers would remain resignedly though uncomfortably standing in this rigid tableau of readiness. For it was well known among Sade's men that the slightest deviation from his orders could and often did cost the miscreant his life. Sade may have been more of a woman than a man in bed with the pretty boys he preferred over women, but he was the most savage of men when it came to meting out punishment.

Still sitting on his human divan, luxuriously softened by two fat pillows strapped to the boys' slender backs, Sade watched the arrival of a wagonload of casks of oil. He smiled, his eyes shifting from the oil to the long formation of archers and then to the black gaping mouth of the cave. The smile turned into a mean grin. The fun was about to begin.

A delicately featured aide of some twenty-odd years sauntered up beside the general. "Perhaps the time has come for you to speak to the rebels, your eminence."

Sade nodded, affectionately slapped the youth's round bottom under his short tunic and rose.

The long line of archers tightened like a drawstring as Sade bearishly strode in front of them to the cave entrance, stopping far enough to dodge any hurled missile but close enough to be heard inside.

"Come out and live!" he shouted to the trapped rebels. "Or stay and die! The choice is yours. You have only five minutes to decide!"

The fifteen insurgents inside were chilled by Sade's ultimatum. It was like the voice of doom, booming, inexorable and without a modicum of human compassion. For the most part they were simple, hardworking young farm boys. Their clothes were in tatters from the last fray with Cromwell's soldiers and they carried crude, homemade weapons—pitchforks, shovels, picks, scythes and hand axes. But they were far from being stupid. The option Sade had given them was no option at all. They had no illusion of being spared if they went outside, for everyone knew Cromwell had issued a blanket order to hang, quarter or in any other way kill every last one of the rebels. And if they chose to remain inside it was only a matter of time before Sade's soldiers stormed the cave and crushed them by sheer force of numbers.

With the exception of Kabal, posted to guard the mouth of the cave, the rebels were assembled a good distance inside Skull Cave, most of them standing. Torches held by a dozen men filled the cave with weaving and elongated shadows of their figures, and the orange flames highlighted the fatigue, anger and hopelessness on their glistening faces.

"Well," Rodrigo, their hotheaded leader, addressed his men. "You heard the jackal outside. Do we fight or do we surrender?"

He was as lean and slick in movement as he was agile with his sword. He was twenty-eight and older than most of these stripling but dedicated soldiers. For a while he had been pressed into Cromwell's army. He stayed only long enough to master the art of soldiery, instantly deserting when he heard Mikah was mustering a rebel force. Having witnessed firsthand the barbarous cruelty inflicted upon his fellow Eh-Danians under Cromwell's reign, he despised the tyrant king with every fiber of his soul. As for the question he had just tossed his men, it was purely rhetorical, for he was certain of their answer.

"I repeat, do we surrender or fight?"

A murmur spread among' the rebels, rapidly swelling into a chant, which exploded in one unified cry of, "Fight! Fight! Fight!"

Rodrigo almost broke into tears with heartfelt pride in these makeshift, inexperienced warriors. What they lacked in expertise they made up for a thousandfold in valor—and it would be a privilege to die with such brave men.

Now that the rebels unanimously agreed to a last ditch fight they worked themselves into a lather of battle-readiness by shouting war cries, jumping up and down and rattling their puny weapons over their heads. They would have continued in this vein had not a shriek from Kabal at the mouth of the cave broke through the din, instantly silencing them.

"Oil!" Kabal shrilly cried, rushing into view, terror stamped on his callow face, for he was only seventeen. "They're pouring oil outside the cave!"

"Dogs!" Rodrigo bellowed, grabbing a homemade spear of flint and wood from the nearest rebel. "Wait here, men!" he commanded, dashing to the front of the cave and flattening his back against the sweating wall. He peered slowly out of the cave like a turtle lifting its head out of its shell.

Damn! Just as Kabal had reported, there in front of an impregnable wall of Red Dragons was one of the notorious pederast's boy vassals, pouring oil in the form of a long black snake in front of the cave, and it was slowly creeping toward the cave entrance. Sade planned to roast them alive. There was no time to hesitate.

Rodrigo's sure hand gripped the middle of the spear and he leaped into full view of Sade and his men just long enough to hurl the spear at the vassal and run back inside. The spear shot through the air like a bolt of lightning, piercing the boy's ribs and vitals. His screams were earsplitting as he fell on the sand flaying his arms and legs like a crippled insect. Rodrigo had acted so fast that the archers didn't have time to fire. His men cheered and clamored about their leader.

Outside, Sade was erupting like a volcano. Furiously marching back and forth in front of his archers, he gesticulated wildly while rebuking them. "Asses! Donkeys! Toads! You let that slippery eel escape!"

He now turned his wrath upon the two frightened vassals cowering by the wagonload of oil. They were trembling and couldn't unglue their eyes from their comrade twitching in the sand with a spear sticking out of his shattered ribs. "Don't just stand there—fools! Pour more oil!"

Fearing the same fate that had befallen their friend, they panicked and tore off hysterically down the beach, away from the scene.

"Feather the cowards!" Sade shouted, and a dozen archers broke formation to discharge a volley of zinging arrows after the fleeing youths. They toppled forward and hit the sand on their faces, arrows still quivering in their backs.

Sade now climbed onto a boulder overlooking the cave and the Red Dragons, marking that the spilled oil had already snaked to within twenty feet of the cave. "There's enough oil to do the job! Prepare to light your arrows!"

The Red Dragons lowered their bows and arrows as one of the torchbearers ran to each man and ignited the tip of his arrow.

Behind another cluster of boulders in the sand, not far from the wagonload of oil, Talon had watched the daring rebel's spear throw, the senseless slaying of the fleeing youths, and now the eerie spectacle of the torching of arrows. One by one the tips of the deadly missiles flared into life and soon a hundred separate flames danced in a long row like fire spouting from the heads of the archers. It would have almost been pretty had not Talon known the grisly purpose of those arrows. The moment that sliding river of oil reached the cave Sade would give the order to fire—and the interior would become an inferno. If he was going to do anything at all he had to act fast. But what in the name of Jove or the new Christian God Christ could he do? He was only one man against a hundred of the most feared archers in the world. Moreover he wasn't even carrying his tribladed sword; it was strapped to his horse back in the city with Darius and the rest of his men.

"This is your final chance!" he heard Sade threaten the rebels. "Surrender now or roast!"

Talon flogged his mind in search of an answer

to this dilemma. Then his eyes alighted upon the wagonload of oil again and he smiled. How went the old saying? "Sometimes one must fight fire with fire."

Sade felt hot blood course through his veins. The prospect of witnessing the devastation of large numbers of men always excited him; an excitement that was almost akin to how he felt when buggering some comely lad. He looked from the shimmering glow encompassing the Red Dragons from the flaming arrows and he was very pleased with them. They looked fierce, invincible, handsome. "Ready!" he shouted, and the archers raised their bows again to the proper trajectory. "Aim and fi—"

His sentence was cut short by the wagonload of oil suddenly hurtling toward his men at breakneck speed—as if being pushed by an unseen force. A rope on fire was tired to one of the casks of oil. The next second the wagon rammed into the battle line and exploded into a billowing holocaust of fire, shooting up into the sky and engulfing most of the archers. Sade was nearly sucked into the conflagration himself, for a long arm of fire reached for him on the boulder, but he jumped out of its grasp to the sand.

But most of his men were not so lucky. They had become human torches and were now either rolling in the sand or running into the ocean to extinguish the fire. The sound of their screams and the sizzling of flesh coupled with the flapping and belching of flames was deafening.

As Sade lay on his belly in the sand watching this incandescent horror and confusion, he noticed the band of rebels cautiously nosing out of the cave to observe the fiery chaos. And as if it weren't humiliating enough to see his own men turning to cinders, the rebels started to laugh and cheer.

Sade scrambled to his feet and looked left and right down the enflamed shoreline, wondering which way to run. It was then that the long shadow of a leaping figure crossed the periphery of his vision. When he looked in the direction of the shadow he saw a very large man standing on top of the highest boulder, his muscular legs spread wide apart, his arms akimbo and his thickly tressed head thrown back in an eruption of raucous laughter. The swine was derisively laughing at the destruction of his beloved Red Dragons. To add insult to injury he heard the rebels join him in the mockery.

"Ho, all you rogues and rascals!" he shouted to the rebels who were still more in than outside the cave. Talon made a general motion toward the half-dozen dazed archers who had survived the flames. "Do you expect me to do all your killing? Come outside and split some skulls!"

Rodrigo signalled that his men obey the stranger and the motley warriors came charging out of the cave to quickly vanquish the straggling archers—but sparing the handful of weaponless vassals.

Sade watched this perverse turn of events, at first incredulously and then going mad with murderous rage. He yanked his sword into view and went scaling and cursing up the boulders to the one where Talon held fast. Below, beyond the still roaring fire, the rebels looked up at Sade and the grinning barbarian who had saved their lives.

They were enthralled with the clash that was about to take place between these two titans, the firelight silhouetting their bodies with a grotesque glow.

As Sade crouched and stalked the seemingly fearless and mocking young hulk, he kept inching away, moving circularly. Occasionally he would take a whack at the handsome dog with his sword but missed; the youth moved with the speed of quicksilver. If he could only take that youthful head back with him to Cromwell perhaps the king would not deal too harshly with him for his defeat here. "I don't know who you are or how you did this," he said, gesturing toward the flapping flames, "but you'll pay for your tricks, pig!"

He swung his sword at Talon again, but Talon ducked. As the sword whistled over his head Talon kicked the blade out of Sade's hand and immediately grabbed him by his sprained wrist with one hand, wedging his other one between the general's legs. With one swift lift he hoisted Sade high over his head with the ease of lifting a child. The rebels below murmured in awe of this show of strength.

"To h-e-l-l with you!" Talon droned out, as he hurled Sade into the cauldron of fire below.

The rebels were ecstatic to see the murderous and depraved Sade dispatched this way and they cheered Talon accordingly. But when a number of overly enthusiastic rebels started to climb the boulder to embrace and thank him, he jumped down to the sand and began rapidly walking away from the fire. He wasn't up to being fawned over or extolled, and the image of sweet Alaña and the question of how to depose Cromwell still overshadowed whatever he had accomplished here. Besides, he still faced the challenge of liberating Alana's brother and he had better get on with it. Certainly these young, bedraggled insurgents weren't going to do him any good; they looked as if they had been through ten sieges in a row and needed a week's sleep. He would enlist his own men for the rescue of Alana's brother—that is *if* he could locate the particular brothel they were no doubt whoring in.

But the euphoric rebels would not let him escape so easily. They surrounded him, blocking his path and showered him with praise. Rodrigo pushed his way through the milling crowd to the stranger. "Please wait, sir!" he implored. "We owe you our lives! How can we ever repay you?"

"For the moment, by getting out of my way. I have another equally important mission to handle."

Rodrigo motioned that the throng part and Talon continued along the beach. But Rodrigo walked by his side, determined to find out more about this mysterious man. The rest of the rebels trailed close behind the pair, both Talon and Rodrigo taking long, measured strides.

"I'm Rodrigo, leader of this group of rebels. Who are you, my friend?"

Talon kept up the fast pace, still reluctant to break his anonymity.

Rodrigo was perplexed by this handsome warrior's reticence to talk. But all the great leaders were known to be moody and unpredictable. And there was no doubt in his mind that this young man of wonders could prove to be the decisive catalyst in overthrowing Cromwell. Or was he already in Mikah's and Alana's service?

"What should we do?" Rodrigo asked, suspecting that the stranger just might have orders from the heir apparent to the throne.

"Whatever you want."

"But don't you have any orders for us from Mikah?"

Talon felt a little eddy of warmth inside his chest at the mention of Mikah. He had not seen his childhood friend in more than eleven years. Would they recognize each other when they finally did meet? "From Mikah? No. None."

Rodrigo was crestfallen. The inscrutable and imperious-looking warrior obviously wished to be left alone. Rodrigo stopped, as did his men. But Talon forged ahead without once looking back.

Still Rodrigo could not let this potentially invaluable ally slip away so easily. "Take us with you, sir!" he shouted after him. "I'm sure we're on the same side!"

"Go home!" Talon shouted back. "Your men look starved, tired and in dire need of rest! You'll fight another day!"

Rodrigo and his men stood watching the proud stranger fade into the night, bewildered and disappointed. Kabal, the young sentry who had guarded the mouth of the cave, pushed up beside Rodrigo.

"Where's he going?" he asked his leader.

"Into another battle, I suspect. Did you not hear him say, 'I have another equally important mission to handle'?"

"Did he say anything about what we should do?" the youth persisted.

"He told us to go home. I think he believes we're too battle-weary to be of service to him."

Rodrigo turned around and faced his ragged band of improvised soldiers. "What say you, men?

101

Are we too weak and sissified by war to be of service to the man who saved our lives?"

"*No!*" they roared back in unison.

"Then let's hurry after him or we'll miss out on the rebellion!"

Eleven

FROM THE OUTSIDE, WITH ITS gleaming gold walls and Gothic spires piercing the midnight heavens, Cromwell's castle was the epitome of serenity in stone. Built on a base of solid rock, commanding an uncluttered sweep of somnolent Elysium below, surrounded by a huge moat where ivory swans sailed during the day, there was nothing in the tranquil facade of this magnificent pile to indicate that anything untoward or cruel ever occurred inside its prodigious bulk. Most of the tall arched windows were dark at this late hour. But even the few that remained torchlit suggested an impregnable haven of peace and rest.

In reality, deep within the sweating stone bowels of the castle, where there was always more darkness than light, manmade horrors were manufactured all the time, even as they transpired now, belying the citadel's outward appearance of cozy bonhomie.

The whisper of diaphanous veils, a whiff of perfume, and the sight of curvaceous flesh was rare in this part of the castle. But the exotically beautiful harem girl who sinuously moved through it now seldom had cause to come here.

Elizabeth hated descending the spiraling stone steps to the gloomy dungeons below the castle's upstairs opulence. They were scary and crawly with roaches and rats. Besides, ever since she was a little girl and had been given by her parents to the harem-mistress she had been a concubine, not a common slave girl. Which was why she so resented bearing a silver tray of carafes and ornate goblets of wine to the dungeons tonight. The girl regularly assigned to these menial duties was sick and she had been snared into substituting. That was why she wore veils and hardly anything more underneath, rather than the boring robes the ordinary slave girls wore. The only gratification Elizabeth received from these rare occasions when she visited the dungeons was the pleasure of seeing lust in the eyes of the guards when they saw her. If she was in a generous mood, Elizabeth might even let one of the guards cup one of her ample breasts or run a finger on the outside of her bushy cleft.

As she descended lower into the bowels of the castle Elizabeth tried to stop her ears to the moans and sporadic screams of the prisoners in the numerous cells. Poor dears. King Cromwell was bestially cruel, that was for sure. And he carried his taste for pain with him into the harem in the form of a short mean whip. But what could a poor girl like her do but submit to anything he desired of her, along with praying that the rebels would one day eject Cromwell from the throne?

As Elizabeth approached the huge iron door that led to the torture chamber, two thoughts flashed through her mind; the prisoner inside had to be very important indeed for the king himself to visit him at this late hour—and who could he be?

She raised the knocker and banged three times, metal on metal resounding throughout the dungeons. The door creaked open and Victor, the rough but well-endowed guard, ushered her inside, winking as she slid into the musty gloom.

A single bowl of fire on a mossy block of stone was the only light in the shadowy torture chamber. But there was no mistaking the king in his royal red cape, gold breastplate and hair like yellow wool. Nor did she have to strain her eyes to recognize the terrifying presence of Verdugo, the Royal Torturer; his large shaved head and massive bare arms and bare chest under a short leather vest often appeared in her worst nightmares. But who was the wretched young man strapped on two wooden crosspieces, his beautiful chest glistening with sweat and smears of blood and bruises, his brown soulful eyes mirroring hideous tortures just lived through?

"So, *Prince* Mikah," Cromwell jeered the young man on the crossrack, "are you ready now to tell me the whereabouts of Xusia?"

Elizabeth had to bite her lips to keep from gasping. Mikah! The leader of the uprising himself! The torturer and the sad prince watched Cromwell whisk one of the goblets off the tray and down the wine to its dregs in one lusty gulp. How she wished she could comfort Mikah's parched lips with wine too!

Cromwell grabbed a second goblet and motioned that Elizabeth leave the chamber. "Out, harlot. And say nothing of what you've seen here tonight—or you too will end on the rack!"

"My lips are forever sealed, my lord!" she vowed and scurried out of the torture chamber, hardly able to contain herself until she told the harem who was held prisoner below them.

Perhaps it was the residual pain of having had his arms stretched from their sockets or the sulpherous sting of lashes across his back, but Mikah had difficulty understanding what the tyrant was talking about. "Xusia? I don't know what you're saying."

"Come, come, Mikah. How else could this rabble uprising have come this far? Xusia's powers and evil genuis must be behind it. He is the only one who is equal to challenging me."

Some dim light of comprehension came into Mikah's salty eyes. "If you're referring to the sorcerer, Xusia of Delos supposedly died a thousand years ago." Then he added sarcastically, "Is it possible that the mighty Cromwell is frightened by a myth?"

The King scowled and slapped Mikah across the face. "Don't get flippant with me, boy! I am not some superstitious shepherd. I myself raised Xusia from the dead." He cracked his knuckles with anger directed at himself. "Little did I know what I let loose upon the world!"

The slap had the bite of a butterfly compared with the pain Mikah had already suffered. And he'd brook a lot more pain if that was the price he had to pay for getting Cromwell's goat. "A wild tale you tell, outlaw king!"

Driven by ire and frustration, Cromwell paced frantically back and forth in front of Mikah and the Royal Torturer. Verdugo scratched his huge shaved dome, filled with misgivings and confusion. He had never seen the king act this way. He had always thought the king was a man of steel. Nothing could bend him until now.

"It is no tale, I assure you! I have stalked Xusia for eleven years watching for signs of his handiwork. When you and Alana were snatched from beneath my blade, I knew that Xusia was going to use you against me. And he *has* been using you two as pawns to usurp my kingdom, hasn't he?"

"*Your* kingdom?"

"Dammit, boy, accept things as they are! I am the king and you are not! And don't pretend you know nothing of what I speak!"

"I cannot believe what you're saying. All this talk of Xusia and bringing him back to life. What kind of a game are you playing with me?"

Cromwell suddenly halted in front of Mikah, bringing his face close to his. The tyrant who was notorious for masking any sign of emotion was falling apart before his very eyes.

"Are you blind, Mikah, to the menace before us all? The signs are visible everywhere. The earthquakes, the plagues, the locusts. And haven't you heard of the virgins disappearing from the villages? Or the howling and shrieking echoing up from graves? The heads of pigs and disemboweled carcasses litter the roadside. Have you been so busy trying to topple my throne that you haven't heard of all this?"

"I don't know about the earthquakes and plagues, but if there are virgins missing and animals senselessly mutilated I suspect your own Black Klaws are responsible."

"Ass!" Cromwell exploded, continuing to fulminate in front of Mikah. "My god, man, I tell you

107

there's a demon in our midst and I know he is the leader of your cause! Now tell me where he is and I may spare you and your sister!"

The ropes on Mikah's wrists were cutting into his flesh but he managed to puff out his chest and proudly throw back his head. "I, and I only, am the leader of our glorious rebellion!"

Cromwell would not be placated. "Very well. Perhaps you don't know Xusia's real identity. He may be posing as your mentor or advisor."

"There is no such person."

"He might not look like a demon. In human form, he could look like anyone. But there would be traces of a serpent in his face or the wildness of a jackal in his eyes."

Mikal was suddenly weary of all this absurd talk about sorcery, plagues and lycanthropy. His body was shot through with thumping aches and searing pain, and death was a large black bird hovering over him. "There is no one leading the revolution but me, I said!" He was monumentally tired and resigned to whatever be his fate. Cromwell had obviously gone quite mad.

Cromwell threw his goblet against the wall, splashing wine on himself. "Verdugo!" he shouted to the Royal Torturer. "Go again at the dog!"

But Verdugo no sooner reached for the crank on the rack when the chamber door flew open, admitting a guard practically carrying a badly burned and blooded Red Dragon. One arm around the archer's waist, he dragged him in front of Cromwell. The king scrutinized the obviously dying soldier, fearing the worst kind of news. "What's this?" he demanded.

"Skull Cave." Spittle dribbled from the corners of his mouth as the archer labored to speak. "The rebels escaped. . . . The Red Dragons—no more!"

Mikah's face lit up. Hope surged through his pain-racked body again. Perhaps the rebellion would succeed yet!

Cromwell was beside himself with rage. He grabbed the straps of the archer's empty quiver and shook him violently. "My Red Dragons destroyed! Be specific, damn you!"

Somehow the rapidly expiring archer found the strength to speak. "A giant barbarian . . . with a steel hand . . . appeared from nowhere. He was a beast—a demon. . . . He conjured fire out of the sky and set us all aflame! It was awful . . . The charred flesh! Men running into the ocean to drown! Awful! Then night became day . . . the rebels turned into wild men, chopping heads, legs, hands. Then . . . then—"

He died with Cromwell still shaking him. When the king released him the archer collapsed on the filthy stone floor.

Cromwell was convinced that the so-called "barbarian" the Red Dragon had referred to was in reality Xusia. The sorcerer's magic enabled him to assume any form, man or beast. He was convinced too that Mikah knew this as well. He shot an accusing finger a few inches from Mikah's eyes. "It's the work of Xusia again—isn't it, *prince*? Your vile leader!" He faced the guard who had brought the archer into the torture chamber. "Throw his carcass to the dogs and double the guards in the castle!"

Cromwell drew close to Mikah again and adopted a more conciliatory mien. "Mikah, listen. It's not just for my life that I fear Xusia. He's an utterly depraved, power-hungry monster—more

109

beast than human. Unless I find him he will wreak havoc upon us all—including the Eh-Danians you claim you love so much. For the love of mankind itself, I beg you to tell me where I'm likely to watch the barbarian—for I know, as you know, that he is in actuality the sorcerer!"

Mikah sighed with powerlessness, steeling himself for the next round of torture he knew would inevitably come. There was no reasoning with Cromwell. This obsession with a sorcerer coming back to life to plague him had unhinged Cromwell's mind. "I know nothing either of the barbarian or your alleged sorcerer!"

"Tear the flesh from his bones!" Cromwell shrieked at Verdugo, who at once and with alacrity began to crank the cross-rack that would stretch Mikah's muscles another inch.

"Do as thou wilt—Cromwell!" Mikah snapped back at him, with every drop of venom he could pour into the shout. "It won't change my answer or save your ass! Your downfall is written in the stars! Your—aaaaahhh!" A tendon ripping cut short the denounciation.

Twelve

BENEATH THE SAVAGE MOUNTAIN RANGE that girded Elysium was a subterranean world of bubbling, flaming tar pits and caverns. It was a world known only to Eh-Dan's handful of wizards and witches, and its entrance was kept tightly secret.

Because of its fanglike stalactites and stalagmites, the largest of these caverns resembled the wide-open mouth of a dragon, and the tongues of fires that shot up from its moat were like the dragon's fiery breaths.

It was to this cavern that Xusia had retreated for rest and reflection ever since the day eleven years ago when he reassembled the atoms of his own body after Cromwell had ripped it open. Here was where Xusia contemplated bizarre lessons of pain and humiliation for Cromwell, his betrayer. And plotting the abhorred king's final and inglorious annihilation became the sorcerer's *raison d'être*—and he cared not one whit how many innocent people were victimized in order to peel the skin and meat from Cromwell's abominable bones!

These were some of the dark thoughts Xusia had shared aloud many times with Roba—the young witch who had left her livelihood of reading Tarot cards and making sterile women fertile to service Xusia, her beloved master. Roba watched over him while he slept, cooked his inhuman meals for him and willingly submitted her body to the punishment of his bestial organ whenever his passions roared for her.

Roba was lounging on the stone steps that led to the massive granite throne where Xusia now slept. Cupping her pointy breasts through a long black robe, to amuse herself while the sorcerer slumbered, she imagined the leaping and weaving flames in the moat encircling the steps to be the virgins Xusia had had her abduct and have carnal perversion with—while the sorcerer had watched, cackled and fondled himself. But while these imaginings excited her greatly, and though her eyes were green-wild on drugs, her cat's ears were ever attuned to any foreign sound that might intrude upon her master's sleep. From time to time Roba would lovingly glance up at Xusia's leathery reptilian features, then return to staring into the fire. How blessed she was to be the master wizard's chosen acolyte!

The rattle of a sword in its sheath instantly galvanized her to her feet. She trained her blazing green eyes in the direction of the intrusion. Then, through the haze of smoke and fire Roba saw the spy Xusia had planted among the rebels, Ninshu. He was stumbling toward the drawbridge across the fiery moat and one of his arms hung limp at his side, bearing an ugly dry wound. Roba jumped in front of the bridge and blocked his way, hissing at him because she would not permit her master's sleep to be broken, and because she distrusted all spies on general principle.

"Stop!" she hissed again. "Thou shall not disturb our Dark Father! He is in his Black Sleep!"

Ninshu stormed across the bridge and pushed her aside. She fell on the steps. "Out of my way, witch! I have business with Xusia and Xusia alone!"

Roba crouched on the steps like a cat ready to spring, pondering whether to rush Ninshu into the fire. Then a smug smile twisted her thin blue lips. Let the idiot spy disturb the master's sleep. Xusia's wrath would be far worse than anything she could do to him.

Ninshu dropped to his knees at the foot of Xusia's thrown and, in the most obsequious and urgent of voices shouted, "I implore you, lord and master of all things powerful, forgive my intrusion!"

Xusia shuddered and his hooded eyes flickered open, his wide slit of a mouth curling contemptuously when he saw who had dared violate his much needed sleep. For powerful as he was he had been working his magic hard and even a sorcerer must sleep.

"Master," Ninshu hurried on. "Cromwell has clipped the balls of the rebellion!"

"How so?" Xusia demanded. It was bad enough to have his sleep shattered but to be awakened to such news was unforgivable!

"He has taken Mikah prisoner. Reports are that he has also captured Alana."

The perpetually exploding flames behind Ninshu were not nearly as awesome as the red glow of hate that bathed Xusia's churning features now.

"Thou art a blundering pile of flesh!" the sorcerer railed. "I should never have entrusted thee as my spy amongst the rebels!"

Ninshu knew his life was in danger and he quaked with fear. "It was not my fault, master! Somehow Cromwell learned of our plans!"

Xusia stared at the groveling, bedraggled spy with unmitigated scorn. Cromwell's men must have recognized Mikah on the street and followed him to the rebels' lair. But to learn that his carefully laid plans had been foiled by a fluke from such scum as Ninshu was insufferable. Besides, he had no further use for the spy. "You dare bring me such outrageous news, dog! Without Mikah the revolt has lost its cause!"

Xusia raised one of his hands and made a beckoning gesture toward the long streaming flames in the moat, as if he were summoning trained serpents. Instantly several of the flames leaped out of the moat to lap at Ninshu's flesh. He jumped and shrieked with pain, while Roba clapped her hands with vindictive glee. "Mercy!" he begged, slapping at the flames curling around him as if they were indeed attacking serpents. "It must have been Machelli who betrayed Mikah—not me, master! He talked last with the prince!"

For some reason this information angered Xusia even more. "Machelli! You are dumber and more stupid than I thought!"

Xusia raised his hand to the flames again and this time a wall of raging fire surged for Ninshu, enveloping and sucking him into the moat with one belching roar. He squealed like a pig being roasted alive. Roba rushed to the edge of the moat to watch him burn. "Good riddance, master!" she yelled through her own maniacal laughter.

Once Ninshu's irritating squeals subsided the sorcerer did not give him a second thought. Besides, his eleven-year obsession to crush Cromwell quickly returned to push everything else from his mind. In the light of the recent turn of events it was clear that he had to depend less on the rebels and more on himself to best the renegade king and his betrayer.

Xusia rose from his throne of granite, adjusted his long, sweeping robes and moved down the steps, shouting to Roba, "Leave your entertainment, witch, and make arrangements for the boat. Now I must finish the business at hand!"

Thirteen

THE SEWAGE SYSTEM UNDERNEATH Elysium was badly in need of repairs, as was most everything else in this plundered and sorely neglected city under Cromwell's reign. Made up of a maze of long, twisting tunnels, caverns and sloshing rivulets of human filth and water, parts of this subterranean labyrinth were drying up but still slimy and overpoweringly odious.

It was through one of these drier but slippery sections of the sewer world that Talon and Rodrigo led the band of rebels from Skull Cave, trudging closer and closer to the castle grounds above.

The only light here came from the dozen flaming torches distributed among the men. Rodrigo carried one of them. And the tricky and illusory play of shimmering light and pulsating shadows on the walls often hindered rather than helped moving over the treacherous ground. At no time did they ever see more than ten feet in front of them, while the uneven rock formations frequently caused the band of warriors to crouch, stoop and come close to crawling on their bellies.

For Talon, being the largest man in the bunch, these cribbed confines were even more difficult to negotiate than for the others. More than once he bumped his head on an unsuspected overhanging rock. Nor did carrying the small cask of oil under his arm make walking over the slippery terrain any easier.

As Talon rounded a bend in the tunnel he lost his footing and nearly went down. "Damn it, Rodrigo! Is this the only way into the dungeon? It stinks—in more ways than one!"

"We can't possibly get in from the top side, my lord."

"Don't call me that!" It embarrassed him to have a man approximately his own age address him with such reverence. Besides, from the moment they met he had taken an instant liking to Rodrigo and considered him an equal.

"Then what should I call you?" Rodrigo asked.

Talon still did not think the time was ripe to disclose his real identity. "For the time being call me T."

"T?"

"Yes, T. How much—" His sentence was cut short by bumping into another overhanging rock. "What a place!"

Rodrigo and the others laughed at his clumsiness, rendered all the more funny because it was in marked contrast to the grade and deftness he had displayed at Skull Cave. But the friendly laughter did not offend Talon because during their short interval together an air of humorous camaraderie had developed between Talon and the young rebels.

117

"It's not much further. In fact, I hear the stream that leads to the castle moat. Our exit is only a short distance from where the stream meets with this sewer."

Suddenly Talon froze in his tracks, the action bringing the rebels to a halt too.

"What is it?" Rodrigo asked, alarmed by the grave concern on his new friend's face.

Talon motioned for him and the others to be quiet. A current of uneasiness went through the rebels as Talon cocked his ears to pierce the inky blackness behind them. And as he bobbed and tilted his head as if listening to voices no one heard but him, the makeshift soldiers clutched their weapons tighter.

"What do you hear?" Rodrigo whispered.

Instead of replying Talon cuffed his steeled hand over Rodrigo's handsome mouth. *"Listen!"*

Silence prevailed once more in the caverns, a silence so pure that every gurgle of the sluggishly flowing sewage nearby was heard with magnified keenness.

Then the sound that Talon had been the first to register became audible to everyone. It came rushing at them from out of the rocky corkscrew interiors through which they had already passed. And as the noise sharpened, the horror on each man's face bespoke the same recognition; what they were listening to was the muted whir of thousands of squeaking and scurrying rats.

"Run!" Talon shouted, and the rebels shot off like arrows into the darkness lying ahead. In their panicky flight from the stampeding, hunger-crazed rodents they jostled and shoved each other in tight narrow spaces, slipped and fell in other

118

spots, only to resume running at breakneck speed. Their flashing torches cast riotous shadows of themselves on the sweating walls, racing alongside with them. But regardless how fast they ran they knew that sooner than later the rats would overtake them. It was only a matter of time before what must look like a rippling carpet of rats would sweep around one of the tunnels to engulf them.

Struggling vainly to keep up with the young rebels was Cornellus, one of the few elderly men who had early thrown in their lot with the young hotbloods. His torch shaking violently as he pumped his increasingly weakening legs, Cornellus was falling behind the fleeing pack. But the prospect of those vile creatures crawling all over his body drove him on, even as he began to stumble and grind to a leaden pace.

The rebels were a good twenty yards ahead of Cornellus when Kabal—the baby of the squad—glanced over his shoulder and saw the plight of the old man. Cornellus had been like a father to him. Kabal swallowed his terrible fear of rats and doubled back to retrieve his aged mentor. Cornellus grabbed Kabal's outstretched hand—the old man's gray eyes teary with gratitude—and let the brave boy pull him along as they ran together. But they only dashed a short distance when Cornellus' overworked legs began to wobble and falter. He just could not run any more.

"Save yourself, son!" Cornellus shouted, relinquishing Kabal's hand and motioning him to go ahead.

Kabal ignored Cornellus' exhortation and lost no time in hooking the old man onto his back.

Cornellus held his torch with one hand while locking his arm about Kabal's chest and the boy sprinted after the others, who were rapidly fading in the distance.

The flaming torches made the fleeing rebels look like the tail end of a comet. Kabal wanted to yell out to them, "Please wait!" But he would not act cowardly, regardless of their fate. So he continued running with the burden of the old man on his back, though in his heart he already knew he would never be able to catch up with them.

"Drop me and go on alone!" Cornellus begged. But Kabal's arms only tightened under his tired old legs.

"Never, father! Together we live or together we die!" Onward he ran, hoping Cornellus did not smell the piss running down his own legs or feel the cold fear numbing his muscles.

The high-pitched sound of the rats was deafening now. They were so close Kabal and Cornellus could smell them. Suddenly, like a raging flood turning a corner, the dreadful noise reached a piercing crescendo. The boy and old man knew the gray tide of death was directly behind them. Fear was a knife cutting into Kabal's legs and he tripped and fell, spilling Cornellus off his shoulders. "Mother!" the boy screamed, covering his face with his arms for the oncoming rats. Cornellus swung the torch around to illuminate the darkness and there, surging toward them, was a ferocious sea of red- and green-eyed rats—their tiny pointed teeth bared as they leaped and proceeded to ravish Cornellus and Kabal in a gory feast of living flesh.

The youth's and old man's screams reverberated throughout the rocky tunnels, driving the rebels up ahead into a mad, headlong panic. They pushed each other aside, trampling the fallen ones beneath the crazed press. Talon and Rodrigo urged them not to succumb to hysteria but they already had. The terror of being devoured by gluttonous rats was greater than any fear of battle.

Talon and Rodrigo pushed their way back through the running rebels, determined to somehow stem the tide of rats rushing toward them.

"Go on!" Talon pushed the young leader in the direction of his disappearing men. He tapped the cask of oil under his arm. "I'll slow the bastards down!" He began to create a pool of oil across the floor of the sweating tunnel.

"I'll stay too!" Rodrigo insisted. Then he heard the final screams of Kabal and Cornellus and his blood turned cold. He decided to take the young giant's advice and ran to join his men.

Talon was about to set the oil aflame when a huge drop of underground moisture from above him fell into the flaming torch, snuffing it out.

"Rotten bastard luck!" Talon howled, tossing the dead torch through the sudden blackness to the rats, who were still swirling atop the remains of the boy and the old man, the reddish glow from Cornellus' torch illuminating the grisly scene. Talon had only one hope: to race to Cornellus' torch, snatch it and get back to the pool of oil before the rats turned on him. And since the torch was no more than twenty feet from the rats he knew he needed luck as much as he needed speed and courage.

He sprinted to the torch, whisked it off the

121

ground and started back just as the feasting rodents finished devouring the last morsel. They now attacked him. Talon used the torch like a swinging sword to repel the first wave of rats, kicking, scorching and stomping to death the dozen rats who got through. The delay gave him time to fling the torch into the pool of oil and run after it, just as the oil exploded into a wall of raging fire, effectively sealing off the rats from the rest of the tunnel and the rebels somewhere on the other side of the fiery impasse.

But by having accomplished this Talon also trapped himself between the fire and the rats now biting at his heels and running up his legs. He had no recourse but to leap through the conflagration, landing and rolling on the ground with several rats still clinging to his cloak and tunic. He rolled frantically on the slimy floor to snuff out the flames that had caught on his clothes while he beat off and used his feet and steeled hand to crush the rats who had survived the fire with him. From the other side of the flames he could hear the rats crawling all over each other in a squeaking frenzy of rage for having lost another meal.

Only slightly seared and bruised, Talon rose, kicked aside the dead rats and tried to see through the roaring sheets of flames to where he knew the skeletons of Kabal and Cornellus now lay.

"Goodbye, brave rebels," Talon said aloud. "Sleep knowing my sword will avenge your death—just as it will avenge my father's death, and my mother's, brother's and baby sister's!"

Talon turned on his heels and ran to catch up with the young rebels, his ears still ringing with the wild squeaks of rats gone berserk.

But as he tore through one tunnel and then down another, he realized he must have taken a wrong turn, for there was no sign of them anywhere.

Fourteen

AFTER SEVERAL TUNNELING HOURS UN-
derground, when Talon pushed open the sewer
door the sudden burst of silvery moonlight hurt
his eyes. But after they got accustomed to the
luminosity he slid out of the tunnel and crawled
on his stomach the short distance to the stream
running into the castle's moat.

Before merging into the water, he lifted his
head just high enough to peer across the moat to
the huge iron door leading to the castle dungeons.
Everything was thus far exactly as Rodrigo had
described it. What he left out, perhaps because he
himself did not know—and, by the way, where
were Rodrigo and his men?—what he had not
mentioned was what looked like a seven-foot,
five-hundred-pound sentry outside the dungeon
entrance. The moonlight sharply defined every
bulging muscle of his enormous naked arms and
massive naked legs. Cromwell's insignia on the
giant's black metal breastplate and yellow plumed
helmet signified that he was one of the king's

Royal Guards. The spear he held at his side was puny compared to his formidable stature. It would take more cunning than ordinary human strength to chop down that huge tree of a man.

Talon slipped into the icy stream—its coldness soothing his blistered skin—and flowed with the stream into the moat, where he swam underwater to the castle side.

When his head bobbed out of the water he gripped the grassy edge of the moat and pondered how to scale and conquer that mountain of muscle guarding the dungeon entrance. The giant stood about fifty yards from where Talon still tread water. It was open terrain on either side of him. There was no way of climbing the embankment unseen and surprising the guard. In the brightness of the night he'd be perceived the moment he emerged from the water.

A soft furry creature, a skunk or a possum, shot across Talon's vision, distracting him from his plight for a second. Talon smiled. Thank you, little creature, Talon thought. The animal gave him an idea. What did possums do when they wished to trick an enemy? Play dead.

Talon pushed away from the embankment. When he reached the middle of the fifty-foot-wide moat, he closed his eyes, turned on his back and let the current from the stream flowing into the moat carry him toward the giant. Talon figured it should take no more than a minute before the formidable sentry noticed what Talon hoped he'd assume to be a dead body.

Eyes tightly closed, the first thing Talon heard was a loud grunt. Then the sound of mammoth legs wading into the muddy shallows of the moat. Talon struggled to keep his diaphragm perfectly still. Now he felt some sharp metal object hook into his cloak—probably the guard's sword or spear—followed by the sensation of being pulled toward shore. Then the sentry's hands grabbed his booted feet and pulled and dragged him up the embankment to the flat ground. He was still holding Talon by the feet when Talon suddenly jackknifed forward and flung his waterlogged cloak over the giant's head and face, kicking himself free of the guard's hands.

"Damn! What's this!" the sentry shouted under Talon's cloak, squirming to untangle himself from its soggy, voluminous folds. "Ahhhh!" he shrieked when Talon's foot crashed into his testes, followed by a merciless volley of smashing fists to his hooded head. The giant doubled over in agony, vomiting all over himself. Talon seized the man's helplessness to wrest his spear off the ground and plunged it clear through the sentry's muscled back. He fell and hit the ground like a building collapsing.

Later, when Talon would reflect upon the moves he made to penetrate the dungeons after slaying the monstrous guard, they reminded him of a series of quick jumps on a chessboard.

Entering the maze of dungeon corridors from the outside, he was no sooner inside when he heard the rattle of armor on a Black Klaw making the rounds and coming towards him. Talon instantly blended with the shadows of a niche in the wall and marked that the sentry was about his same height and build. As the Klaw lazily walked by him, his life was cut short by Talon's rocklike arm shooting about his neck and choking him to death.

126

Minutes later, after disposing of the body in a boiling vat of tar, now dressed in the mail shirt, cloak and helmet of the Black Klaw, Talon continued looking for the dungeon that housed Mikah.

Once again the clink of heavy metal warned Talon of the approach of another sentry. He darted inside a dark but open storeroom and saw, his heart leaping, the sinuous vision of Alana being led by one more Black Klaw. The direction they were moving would take them right past him. She was still in the tattered cloak she wore in the tavern. Talon knew that under it her breasts were still bare. In spite of these grim circumstances a rush of lust went through him at the prospect of one day seeing again and perhaps nuzzling those breasts.

"Where are you taking me?" she dolefully asked, as they marched by Talon.

"Upstairs, sweetmeat," the sentry replied, chuckling coarsely. "The king, I hear, is thinking of making you his bride!"

Alana gasped and cried, "No!" She stopped walking but the Klaw roughly grabbed her by the elbow and pushed her along.

"That's one way of quelling the revolt, isn't it? Marry the leader's sister!" He broke into riotous laughter.

They were now out of Talon's sight but she must have stopped again for he heard the guard urge, "Come on, my queen-to-be. The slave girls have to wash and perfume that pretty body of yours for the king."

Talon remained a few more minutes in the storeroom breathing heavily, raging. His first impulse when he heard of Cromwell's plans for Alana was to run his sword through the sentry and abscond with her into the night. But that would have left Mikah to certain death. For the time being he had to subordinate his personal feelings for Alana to the cause and free her brother first. As for Cromwell making Alana his wife—that would happen when pigs would fly!

Talon shot out of the storeroom and resumed searching for his childhood friend. He was either in one of the cell blocks or on the rack in the torture chamber.

Talon soon found himself facing a large iron door with an open portal. He peered through and saw a long gray cell block. Sitting at a small table next to the door were three sentries engrossed in a game of dice. Mugs and a big flask of wine were on the table and, judging from their flushed faces and their laughter, they looked as if they had imbibed plenty of it. Talon tilted his helmet low on his forehead to partially conceal his features and knocked on the door, his free hand gripping the hilt of the Klaw's sword.

"Shit!" one of the guards exclaimed, vexed by the interruption.

Talon watched the same guard reluctantly rise and glance indifferently through the portal, more of his attention still on the game than the visitor. Clearly he was just another Black Klaw to the guard.

"What is it?"

"I've another prisoner for you."

"Well, hurry up, man. We've got a hot game going."

The moment he threw the bolt back Talon hurled his full weight against the door, sending it flying inward to smash the guard's face, and throwing him against the others. The suddenness and forcefulness of the action sprawled all three of the men on the floor. Before they had the chance to regain their senses, Talon used the heavy hilt of his sword like a club on each man's head, knocking all of them unconscious. He wrested the large ring of keys from the belt of the guard who had unbolted the door, moved into the corridor running between the cells and hurriedly glanced through the portal of each one in search of Mikah.

"Wait!" A familiar voice cried out from one of the cells. "Friend! Warrior! It's me—Rodrigo!"

Talon looked over his shoulder and saw the lean, ecstatic face of the young rebel leader pressed up against a portal. He smiled, moving to the cell. "What the devil are you doing in there?" Behind Rodrigo he saw the rest of the rebels from Skull Cave. They were forced to huddle together because of the smallness of the cell but they were as glad as Rodrigo was to see him.

"We were caught as we exited the sewers," Rodrigo breathlessly explained, anxious for Talon to find the right key to the cell. "They intend to crucify us during tonight's feast."

"I should let them," Talon teased. "It would teach you a lesson for being so clumsy—and for losing me in the sewers."

Talon found the right key, turned the lock and the big clangorous door sprung open. The rebels burst from the cell like water from a breaking dam. The men milled about in the corridor stretching and rubbing their cramped arms and legs. Talon looked down the long row of cells in which the prisoners, now that the rebels were free, clamored for release too.

"Which of the cells holds Mikah?" he asked Rodrigo.

"None, friend. He was taken to the torture chamber. Poor Mikah, after Verdugo gets done with him—he's the Royal Torturer—Mikah may not be alive."

Talon flinched. Pray that were not true! He handed Rodrigo the keys. "Here. Free the others."

Suddenly overcome with weariness from the ordeals he had lived through during the last twenty-four hours, Talon slumped back against the open cell door and watched the squad leader run from cell to cell opening doors. And as he watched the pathetic wretches stagger and limp out of the cells, many of them diseased and emaciated from neglect and lack of food, one part of Talon's mind plotted his next course of action.

In spite of their rundown condition, now that the war and political prisoners were free they experienced a renewal of energy and hope. They flocked around Talon, their benefactor, and inundated him with gratitude and praise. Some of the older and more wasted men even dropped to their knees in front of him and wept. Such an outpouring of affection was too much for Talon to take comfortably.

"Up, for God's sake! You're not animals to grovel! Up, I say!"

Rodrigo was amused by Talon's embarrassment.

Obeying the handsome young warrior who had rescued them, the half-dozen men who had prostrated themselves at his feet now rose. Then a stoop-shouldered, sixtyish old man with flowing white hair and a long beard shouldered his way through the press to Talon. The respect with which the others parted for him revealed that he was either an advisor or spokesman for the prisoners. "We thank you, sir," he said, in a soft, cultured voice.

"For what? We'll probably never get out of here alive!" Talon laughed. He had always resorted to humor or flippancy to cover up embarrassment.

"That may be true, sir—but far better to die as free men than to live as dogs!"

The surrounding prisoners and rebels nodded and murmured agreement.

Talon was enormously impressed by the old man's dignity and courage. "Who are you?"

"My name is Estard Devereux. I was once Cromwell's architect. After I built this very castle in which we stand the king had me incarcerated."

Talon and Rodrigo exchanged flashing looks, both fired by the same idea.

"You say you built this place?" Talon asked with growing excitement.

"Aye. I was locked up five years ago to insure that the castle's secrets would never be disclosed."

Talon's blue eyes blazed. "What secrets?"

Devereux smiled. In the comely form of this young warrior he saw the hope of revenging himself upon the outlaw king at last!

"Why, hidden passages, secret exits and the like," he answered almost coyly.

Talon rested his hands on the architect's frail shoulders, beaming. "Tell me all you know, my friend. I want to hear every delicious little secret at your disposal."

Fifteen

ELIZABETH HAD RETURNED WITH AN-
other tray of wine for Cromwell. She stood
with her pretty head turned away from the
heart-rending sight of Mikah, limp, bloodied and
unconscious. Thank God he was out of it! How
the young Prince had howled with pain as that
hairless brute cranked the rack or whipped his
balls with a wet towel! Conversely, how Cromwell
had hooted and slapped his knees with laughter
each time Mikah discharged blood from his
mouth or nose. And how she wished Cromwell
would get his slimy hand off her ass while he
sipped his wine and leered at the poor Prince.

"How much more do you think the young buck
can take, Verdugo?"

The proximity of hot coals and three hours of
working over Mikah had coated Verdugo's massive body with a sheen of sweat. "Not much, sire."

Someone started impatiently pounding on the
iron door, jarring Cromwell out of his warm, com-
fortable mood. The young wench's ass felt good,

the wine was strong and he had enjoyed the show Verdugo and Mikah had put on for him.

"A pox on whoever dares pound like that!" he shouted to the door.

"Open up, Cromwell! It's me—Malcolm!"

Cromwell's good mood was totally erased now. Malcolm? He had banished him from Eh-Dan ten years ago. His debaucheries with wine, drugs and little girls had scandalized the court, and he was privy to too many of Cromwell's chicaneries and secrets at the time. "Let him in!" he ordered the guard by the door.

Thinner and even more ravaged by drugs and drink than Cromwell remembered him to be, Malcolm strode toward him with a jauntiness of purpose that he had never seen in his ex-chancellor before. His sunken, shadow-rimmed eyes were burning coals, glowing with some maniacal dream. As much as he had come to loathe this wreck of a human being Cromwell was curious to learn what had motivated him to return, knowing his neck was at stake.

"Hello, Titus."

Elizabeth, Verdugo and the guard looked at Malcolm aghast. No one addressed the king by his first name, save the concubines who serviced his untoward pleasures and then only in private. The fact that Cromwell weathered this breach of court protocol without immediately punishing him was even more bewildering.

"What are you doing here? I thought I exiled you."

Malcolm was either too drunk to care or he already knew who hung on the rack, for he ignored Mikah completely and defiantly thrust his bony face toward Cromwell.

133

"I attend the Royal Feast every year, Titus, and it's that time again. But then, how would you know? You're usually away from the feast killing and pillaging."

"Don't taunt me, Malcolm! Your life hangs by a slender thread here!"

Malcolm reached past Cromwell and brazenly tweaked Elizabeth's large nipple through her diaphanous veils, ignoring the king's threat. "I understand, Titus, that the kings of all the bordering nations will also be attending the feast tonight. May I ask why?"

Cromwell glared. Through some evil source the bastard had gotten wind of his plans! "No! You may not ask! Remove him!" he ordered the guard.

The entrance of Machelli, Cromwell's new war chancellor, shifted everyone's focus from Malcolm to him. He had that kind of impact on entering a room, irrespective of how many people were in it. His compelling presence was based on more than just his physical appearance, which with dark suave features, coal-black hair bobbed across a noble brow, piercing black eyes and the whiplike grace of the way he carried himself, was arresting by itself. The charisma he cast was an intangible mix of willfulness, cunning, the potential of evil and yet disarming charm.

As Machelli swept into the Torture Chamber, smoothing out his short black linen cape over a royal tunic edged with gold thread, he wholly ignored Elizabeth and Verdugo but stopped short of the king to appraise Malcolm with unconcealed contempt. "What scum is this?" he asked, pointing a finger at Malcolm as if he were a pile of excrement.

Cromwell was delighted. Machelli was even more cynical and sharp of tongue than Malcolm.

"Why, he's your predecessor, Machelli—a little the worse for wear, perhaps, but your predecessor nonetheless."

Machelli looked at Malcolm again and then smiled at the king foxily. "Is this what is to become of me?"

"Worse, if your interests are not mine." A king remained king by inspiring fear in his subjects.

Malcolm had brooked Machelli's slights in cold silence. But the fury in his eyes left no doubt that he hated the man who now held his former position.

The guard Cromwell had told to usher Malcolm out of the Torture Chamber belatedly snapped to attention and courteously pushed Malcolm toward the gaping door. His general principle was never to be unkind to a nobleman if he could help it, for one never knew when he might be in the king's favor again. "If you please, General Malcolm."

But Malcolm balked at being ejected and shoved the guard's hand off his arm. "I know why you've brought the kings here!" he yelled accusingly at Cromwell, as if he and the king shared a nefarious secret.

Cromwell examined Malcolm carefully. The scoundrel knew something. He had to find out what. He motioned to Machelli, Verdugo and the guard to exit.

"Leave me with this sot." He tried to avoid Machelli's probing eyes. Damn! Now Machelli was suspicious!

"A pleasure to meet you," Machelli addressed
135

Malcolm sarcastically, on his way out, the guard and Verdugo following him.

"And close the door!" Cromwell shouted.

Except for the three half-dead prisoners in a cell at the back of the Torture Chamber and Elizabeth and Mikah, Cromwell was now alone with Malcolm. Mikah was still unconscious so he didn't have to worry about him. As for the tasty slave girl, she was too scared to ever dare tell anyone what she heard here.

Cromwell whisked another gleaming goblet of wine off the tray she held and confronted Malcolm. Their faces were bathed in a reddish glow from the hot iron stuck in a pot of burning coal next to them.

"What do you want, Malcolm?"

"Half the kingdom."

On the surface Cromwell acted as if the demand was the most absurd one he had ever heard. But inwardly his entrails churned with redoubled alarm. Malcolm would never have brazened such an outrageous demand unless he really knew why he was assembling the kings at the feast tonight. "Half! Ha! What sword do you think you hold over me that would be worth half my realm?"

He tried to hide his rapid breathing by taking another gulp of wine and then resumed speaking, all the while only too uncomfortably aware of the gleam of triumph in Malcolm's dissipate eyes. "You're bluffing. You don't have anything over me. The kings are here to celebrate the tenth anniversary of my conquering Eh-Dan, and to sign a treaty of peace. And that's the only reason for this glorious occasion, period."

Malcolm laughed in Cromwell's face. "Bullshit!

136

They're here because they've watched you vanquish Swavia, Goth and Castul. By signing your ridiculous treaty—which we both know is a worthless piece of paper—they hope to avoid the same fate."

"So? Nothing sinister or unusual in a bit of statesmanship, is there?"

Malcolm brought his drawn face close enough to Cromwell's to see the broken blood vessels under his eyes and on his beaky nose.

"Titus, the so-called treaty is only bait to lure them here for a more monstrous reason. And you and I know it."

There was no more point to playing games with Malcolm. He had it figured out correctly. "I'm astonished you can still think after all these years of dissipation," he said ominously.

Elizabeth listened to the terrible tone in their voices, petrified. She didn't understand the meaning behind the words but there was no questioning the hate for each other.

"I can still do a great many things," Malcolm replied threateningly.

Cromwell's mind was a whirlpool of conflicting thoughts. One, however, adumbrated all the others. He could not and would not let this burned-out wretch sabotage the opportunity to expand his kingdom beyond anyone's wildest imagination. "Half is too steep for your silence."

"Really a bargain, Titus, when you consider the stakes."

"But you know nothing!" he shouted, knowing the opposite was true.

"I was your war chancellor and general for many years, Titus. I know you inside and out. Essex, the nobility, the neighboring kings . . .

none of them could ever begin to fathom the depth of the treachery you have in mind for them. But I—"

Elizabeth saw the flash of Cromwell's dagger before Malcolm felt the blade tear through his abdomen into his stomach, where Cromwell twisted it twice before leaving the dagger buried there.

The tray slipped from Elizabeth's hands to the floor as she watched, horrified. Malcolm stumbled backwards to the wall and slid to the floor clutching the dagger lodged in his stomach. The pain was so sharp it choked back his screams. But he did manage to eke out, "Cromwell—you bastard!" A river of blood gushed from his midsection to cover his twitching legs.

Elizabeth remained frozen, incredulously listening to Cromwell laugh at the man who only seconds ago so blatantly taunted him.

But Cromwell's grotesque pleasure was short-lived. Two Black Klaws burst into the Torture Chamber and threw themselves down on their knees before the king, acting as if they were oblivious to the man bleeding to death with the king's dagger in his stomach.

"Sire!" the stouter of the two soldiers shouted. "The dungeon guards are dead and the prisoners have escaped!"

"The gods are pissing on me!" Cromwell thundered, smashing his fist into the other hand. "This too I know is the work of the sorcerer!"

"Losing control, Titus?" Malcolm weakly snickered.

Cromwell swung around and savagely used his foot to push the dagger deeper into his stomach.

Elizabeth squealed at the squishy sound. Malcolm's eyes closed and he died.

Cromwell faced the Klaw who had spoken. "You gather as many men in the castle as you can and meet me at the main tunnel. And you," he nodded to the other soldiers, "come with me!"

Outside the Torture Chamber Cromwell spotted another Black Klaw walking from the latrine at the opposite end of the corridor. "You there!" he yelled. "Kill everyone in the Torture Chamber! Now! On the double!" Neither torture or the fear of death had extracted from Mikah Xusia's whereabouts or his assumed form, so there was no point in letting him live any longer. As for the slave girl or the other prisoners in the Torture Chamber, they had all heard too much of what had transpired between Malcolm and himself.

Obediently, the Black Klaw Cromwell had delegated to do the killing drew his sword and ran into the gloomy Torture Chamber as the king marched away to roust more men.

Inside the rocky chamber of horrors, the Black Klaw chillingly surveyed the instruments of torture; the iron hand crusher, the tongs for ripping out tongues, the tightening iron mask in which so many heads had been crushed like eggs, the assortment of barbed and spiked whips, and the dreadful cross-rack where now hung the tortured and battered body of an unconscious young man. And then he saw the scantily clad young woman lurking in the shadows, her luminous dark eyes fearfully trained on the glittering sword in his hand.

"Do you come to kill me, sir?" she mournfully asked, her tempting breasts heaving in a swirl of revealing veils.

"Fear not," Talon assured her, whipping off his

139

helmet and disdainfully tossing it against the smoke-begrimed wall. "I'm not one of them!"

Elizabeth breathed a sigh of relief and detached herself from the shadows. "Who are you, then?"

"A friend of the Cause." He quickly used his sword to cut Mikah's bindings and caught him as he fell forward, still unconscious. With one heave he slung the lacerated prince over his massive shoulders and, sword still in hand, moved out of the Torture Chamber, beckoning the girl to follow.

"Come with me!"

Sixteen

IT WAS NO EASY TASK for thirteen dog-tired rebels to incessantly dodge a castle full of Black Klaws searching for them. Yet, thanks to the architect Devereux's knowledge of every labyrinthine inch of the castle's layout, including hidden rooms and secret passages known only to him and an esoteric few, for the past hour, since they broke loose from the dungeons, they had been able to do just that.

Still Rodrigo and the others knew they could not press their luck. If Talon did not soon materialize with the catch he had so bulldoggedly set out to bag—Mikah—they would have to pass through the wall panel before which they stood and flee the castle via this secret passage.

The rebels were in an upper wing of the castle overlooking the section where the harem girls were lodged. The alarm gongs and constant sound of amored patrol guards scurrying all around them was nerve-racking.

"I hear soldiers running very close," Rodrigo

whispered to his men. "Be prepared to enter the passage at an instant's notice. Painful as the thought of leaving our rescuer behind is to me—I don't know what else to do! Some of us have to survive or the Cause is lost!"

The younger warriors muttered "ayes" and sadly nodded their heads.

"Look!" Rodrigo exclaimed, brightening.

The others followed his stare. Rounding a corner at the far end of the colorfully bannered hallway was the man who called himself T. Slung over his shoulders was clearly Mikah. A half-dressed slave girl hurried to keep up with the young warrior. He sprinted toward them, so fleet of foot that it appeared Mikah's weight was no burden to him at all.

"You did it!" Rodrigo exclaimed, helping Talon unload the awakening prince from his shoulders. As Mikah rubbed his eyes and wobbled on his feet, Elizabeth and Rodrigo propped him up, careful not to touch any of the terrible lash welts and bruises on his body.

"What did you expect!" Talon laughed, delighted by Rodrigo's ebullience. He gestured to Elizabeth for her to help Mikah into the dark passageway.

Mikah detained her, studying the handsome features of his rescuer with sharpening focus. "I owe you, my friend . . . whoever you are." Some elusive and dim recognition crossed his face. "You look, sir, vaguely familiar. Have we met?"

Talon smiled, squelching the urge to take his childhood friend into his arms and reveal his true identity. This was not the time or the place. "We'll talk about it some other time."

142

"Still I owe you, sir," Mikah insisted, as he let Elizabeth walk him into the passageway.

"No, your sister owes me," he said, remembering Alana's bargain. The words had leaped out of Talon's mouth before he could stop them.

Mikah was confused. "My sister? What do you mean?"

"Nothing." He signaled Elizabeth to move him. "Go. We didn't risk our lives for you only to have you snatched from us so close to freedom."

Elizabeth and Mikah were swallowed into the darkness and the others poured in behind them—all but Rodrigo and Devereux, who were nervously listening to the approach of a patrol somewhere close.

Talon tried to wave them through the open panel. "I'm going to keep the soldiers busy until I'm sure all of you are safely outside the castle."

"I'll stay too!" Rodrigo declared, but plainly wishing he were with his escaping men.

"So will I!" the white-haired architect chimed in, with something less than enthusiasm.

Alone he might be able to divert the guards long enough to assure Mikah's escape. But with these two understandably battle-shy men he'd be slowed down. "Go!" he ordered.

"We get out together or die together!" Rodrigo protested.

Four guards suddenly turned the corner at the far end of the corridor and saw them. "There's some of them!" one of the guards shouted. The patrol raced towards the surprised trio brandishing swords and yelling for reinforcements.

"Well, come on then!" Talon exhorted Rodrigo and Devereux, as he himself charged head on into

143

the oncoming guards without a second thought to his two cohorts.

Because Talon was still dressed in the garb of a Black Klaw the guards were confused, giving him the perfect opportunity to plow into the four men before they realized he was not one of them. With one elegantly orchestrated series of lightning-quick movements, he kicked one guard in the balls, chopped the windpipe of another one with the axlike side of his hand, and drove his head like a bull's into the stomach of a third guard, and tore away most of the fourth guard's face with the steel braces on two fingers of his left hand.

When he turned to see the state of Rodrigo and Devereux he realized they must have taken his advice after all, for they were gone. He smiled. Even the bravest of men has his off days.

He glanced over the four unconscious or dead guards, strewn on the marble floor like broken toy soldiers. Then the approach of many more guards reminded him he was far from being out of danger. He ran to the window at the end of the corridor and stepped through it onto a spiraling stairwell, which led to the roof, many levels above him.

No sooner did he begin to climb than two guards shot through the same window. They took after him in hot pursuit. Talon deliberately slowed down as he ran up the stairs, while their momentum increased. Just as they were virtually breathing down his neck, they raised their swords to cut him and Talon suddenly flung himself at their feet, tripping them with his prostrate body. Giving them no time to recover balance Talon swarmed all over them like an enraged beast, kicking and punching them senseless, and then throwing them down the stone stairs. As they bounced and rolled from step to step blood flew from their heads.

Talon started racing down the stairwell but stopped when he saw the horde of Klaws fill the courtyard below and point up at him. He had no recourse but to go up to the roof, taking three and four steps at a time.

The roof was flooded with moonlight, vividly highlighting the scrollwork and gargoyles on the multitude of turrets and spirals. There was no place to hide and nowhere else to go save over the side. He had run himself into a cul de sac. He had to make a decision regarding what to do at once, for bursting out of a skylight door were fifty or more Black Klaws with his death written all over their hardened faces.

Talon dashed to the edge of the roof and dropped to a narrow ledge about twenty feet below. Above him guards began to pitch spears at him but they flew by him because he was protected by a hollow impression in the wall.

"Get ropes! A ladder!" some soldier on the roof shouted.

Talon pondered the options. Four hundred crashing feet below was the courtyard swarming with soldiers. Above him men were engineering means of reaching him. And about fifty feet below and directly facing him, was the open window of a faintly lit chamber. The window appeared to be his best bet. If he miscalculated he'd go plummeting to a certain death on the stones below. But if he hit his target he would at least buy time against being captured or killed.

Talon pressed his fingertips against the rough stone wall, hunched forward a trifle, rested his weight on his toes, bent his knees slightly and flung himself through the air like a diver soaring from a cliff into the ocean.

His aim was right on target. He dove through the window and landed unharmed on a sea of satin-covered pillows in the harem room, which were littered with a voluptuous tangle of mostly naked concubines. The impact on their bed of pillows startled most of the twenty or so girls awake and they screamed when they saw the wild-looking warrior, scattering into the hallway.

Talon had fallen short by several feet of landing on top of a sleeping blonde. When he raised his head he discovered it was between her spread legs. The girl must have thought she was still dreaming, because, when she languidly opened her eyes and saw the rugged young giant's sensuous mouth so temptingly close to her pink slit, instead of screaming she began to purr and lift her pelvis toward his face.

Talon wished he could oblige the wanton, because the meal she offered was one he had not partaken of in weeks. But there was an outlaw king to dethrone and his own hide was being hunted by hundreds of soldiers at this very moment. So he pulled his head away from between the girl's legs in time to see the girls who had fled the harem room returning. Now that they realized the good-looking warrior meant them no harm they sashayed back to observe him at close range, several of the girls blatantly flirting with him. Talon smiled indiscriminately at the assortment of nubile maids, wishing he could spend a week in this paradise of female flesh sampling them all. But, alas, he couldn't afford another minute here.

Talon leaped to his feet and paused for a moment to kiss the girl on the lips who so obviously wanted him to kiss more. "I'd love to stay, darling—but I really must run!"

And run he did—right out of the harem and into a series of interconnected hallways, finally recognizing the one Devereux had described would take him to the quarters most likely to contain Alana.

He lingered for a moment before the ceiling-high white and gold trimmed door. From inside he heard a flurry of soft female voices making a flattering fuss over Alana's body, for they interjected her name between ooohs and aaahs several times. He backed up about ten feet and then charged forward with his head lowered like a bull's, crashing through the door as if it were a paper bag.

He was so agog by the immediate sight of Alana totally nude on a white linen table, while three beautiful attendants rubbing exotic creams and oils into her skin, that he didn't see the two Klaws off to a side of the room sneaking up on him. Suddenly he was under a merciless rain of fists to his head, ribs and abdomen. He staggered, reeled and, before he realized what the Klaws were doing, they had punched him to the open window and shoved him through it. And as he fell like a stone through the darkness he thought he heard Alana scream, continuing to scream even when he crashed through the thatched roof of the castle's first floor storage room, landing on top of a dozen bags of flour.

The storage room instantly swirled with clouds of the white powder. Talon rose from the broken bags of flour feeling as if he had been stomped by a herd of stampeding horses. He choked and sneezed from the flour in his nose and throat, every bone and muscle of his body aching from the double impact of the fall and the beating he took upstairs. He knew he must resemble a ghost for he was covered from head to toes with flour.

It took him a full minute for his head to stop spinning and when it did, he sprang out of the storage room like a snow-covered bear seeking blood. He couldn't get the two ruffians who had hurled him out the window from his mind and he prayed that he would confront them again face to face. His purpose now was to rejoin the rebels and Mikah but he salivated with desire to smash those and other Klaws along the way.

The chance for revenge arose almost immediately—but it was more than he had bargained for.

Talon was streaking across a moonlit and what appeared to be deserted tile pool courtyard, running toward a maze of tall shrubbery, where he hoped to hide and plan his way out of the castle. Suddenly a cordon of Black Klaws poured out of this same maze from the shadows on either side of him. He was surrounded by a steeled ring of soldiers with himself square in the middle. Here and there in the circle of men he spotted a battered and bloodied face that he had rearranged; the savagery of their glares revealed they were very much hot also to rearrange his face.

The hundred or more Klaws began to tighten around him like a noose. If he was to die here, his spilled blood washed in moonlight, so be it. But he would take many more than one cursed Klaw with him.

The rattle of metal aloft somewhere behind him turned him around. On one of the castle's many balconies directly behind him a line of Royal

Archers stood poised to riddle him with arrows. He smiled. Were the archers really necessary, considering the overwhelming odds already facing him? Or did his unusual achievements at Skull Cave spread rumors that he had superhuman powers calling for extra might?

For some reason the wide circle of Klaws stopped closing, creating a space inside very much like a small arena. What lethal contest did they have in mind for him?

Talon unsheathed the Klaw's sword at his side, whipped out a dagger with his other hand and braced himself for whatever challenge they had in store for him. He spread his muscular legs far apart, thrust his head defiantly forward and waited for the soldiers to make the first move.

In the silvery wash of the night he stood like a primordial beast. And it thrilled him hotly to discern that, in spite of the staggering odds against him, the Klaws were awed and feared tangling with him. And rightfully they should be, for he vowed—on the memory of his slaughtered family— he'd chop down any soldier who came near his blade!

Still the Klaws held back from trying to take him. He began to realize that something more than fear restrained them. They were waiting for someone . . . to do he knew not what.

"Who dies first?" he baited and laughed.

As if on cue, the ranks opened up to admit a fiercely proud-looking man encased in a breastplate and helmet of solid gold. The royal red cape flowing behind him told Talon he was facing the king himself; it had been Cromwell the soldiers had been waiting for.

"I'll be first!" Cromwell raged back, flashing his huge sword in front of him.

Eleven years of seething hate began to boil and overflow Talon's bosom. Cromwell! The killer of his father, mother, baby sister and brother! He tried to harness the tidal wave of anger that threatened to engulf his customarily steely self-control, because he knew if he succumbed to it the scathing emotions would greatly impair his swordsmanship. He also knew he would need all the skills with the blade at his disposal in the duel that was about to transpire. Cromwell's reputation as a swordsman was formidable and far-flung.

"Then kiss the tip of my sword, vile outlaw king!"

The circle of soldiers were riveted with silent fascination to the heroic battle that they knew would take place between these two titans. And now Talon and Cromwell began to circle and eye each other, like two snarling panthers waiting for the right moment to strike.

"Don't act as though you don't know me, Xusia," Cromwell spat out at his adversary. "It's your old friend Cromwell—and the comely form you've assumed does not deceive me!"

Talon had no idea what the king was talking about. He decided he was trying to throw him off balance with this gibberish. "I've been called a lot of names—but never Xusia!"

Cromwell made the first thrust with a stab at Talon's head, missing by only inches. "Let's see what a sorcerer can do against a real swordsman!"

Talon would not allow the sly dog to divert his attention. He slammed his sword powerfully against the king's, the might of the blow clearly shooting pain through Cromwell's wrist. "I'm no sorcerer, royal scum, but test my sword, I beg you!"

Talon dropped on one knee and thrust for Cromwell's belly, ripping his tunic but not his person.

A roar of protests flew up from the soldiers. The young brute was clever and had come too close to robbing them of a king.

The two adversaries were now wholly committed to destroying each other, and the intensity of that commitment burned on their faces like phosphorescence in the moonlight. The air reverberated with the metallic music of their clashing swords, and though the purpose behind their parries and thrusts was lethal, they moved with the gracefulness of dancers.

The brilliant interplay between the two swordsmen worked the Klaws into a lather of excitement. If the towering stranger came close to wounding the king the soldiers booed and grumbled. Conversely, whenever the silky maneuvers of Cromwell brought his opponent to the edge of death, they cheered and clapped their hands. And as the swordfight stretched to five minutes, and five minutes more, the Klaws marveled at the stamina of both men to sustain such a fierce display of energy and skill.

The sweat poured down the young barbarian's flour-streaked face and muscle-rippling arms and legs, making him look like a savage with war paint. Cromwell's own countenance and body glistened with sweat, as they tirelessly continued to exchange blow for blow, sparks flying from their clashing swords like fireflies in the night. The roles of aggressor and defender constantly reversed between them. One second Cromwell

151

would release a dazzle of slices at Talon that nearly blinded him with the speed and fury of the assault. Seconds later Talon would rush the king with a lightning-quick burst of thrusts and cuts that twice resulted in Cromwell falling on his ass, jumping out of the way of his adversary's death-lunge just in the nick of time. Throughout this epic duel, save for a scratch or two, miraculously neither of the truculent warriors suffered so much as a minor wound.

It was after another few minutes that the tide began to turn in Talon's favor.

Though the quality of their swordsmanship seemed equal, Talon had the advantage of youth. Older by at least fifteen years, the king started to visibly tire. And with his arms and legs turning to lead his swordplay grew sloppy and lost elan. Perceiving the king's diminishing capacity, Talon launched his most vigorous attack yet. He hammered and swung blow after blow, forcing Cromwell into an abject retreat. This deluge of murderous strokes culminated in the ring of soldiers parting as Talon drove the king up against the wall. Cromwell's arm pounded with the strain of keeping Talon's relentless assault at bay. He was convinced that if his indefatigable adversary kept up this furious rain of blows his arm would be torn from its socket. His sword felt like a thousand pounds in his hand and he knew that at any moment the young giant would knock it out of his hand.

Cromwell's back pinned against the wall, Talon unexpectedly stopped, backed up to collect his strength, and—his eyes blazing with revenge—like an enraged bull readying for the kill, prepared to charge the king again. Cromwell knew he could not possibly live through another volley of his opponent's brutal blows and deft stabs.

Cromwell was about to cry for his men to save him when Machelli, like a black snake shooting out of the nearest cluster of soldiers to Cromwell, suddenly materialized behind Talon and whipped a long steel-ball mace across the back of Talon's head, sending him crashing to the stones, unconscious.

The crowd of soldiers grunted and wailed with disappointment. They had hoped for a more exciting and gory climax to the tempestuous duel.

Now that Cromwell realized he was safe from this human juggernaut's overpowering superiority, he felt compelled to save face in front of his men by pretending to be angry that Machelli had interrupted the duel. He grabbed Machelli by the collar and violently shook him.

"How dare you intercede! I would have had the young swine's head on the end of my sword by now! I only feigned weakness to throw him off guard!"

Machelli smiled, alert to the king's lies. "Of course, your majesty. But you have no time for this lout," he said, pointing to the huge young warrior sprawled at their feet. "There's not a moment to waste. The rebels are once again at large and you have the Feast of Kings to prepare for tonight!"

Cromwell stuck his sword point against Machelli's throat.

"You dare tell me what to do? No one instructs the king in his responsibilities! I warn you, Machelli—don't overrate your worth to me. Chancellors come and go!"

"My apologies," Machelli said, with mock obsequiousness, "I meant no disrespect. I live only to serve you and to glorify your name!"

"Indeed, Machelli," he replied, not believing a word of it. His chancellor was getting a little too inscrutable and devious for comfort. And if he continued to rouse his suspicions the kingdom of Eh-Dan would most certainly have a new chancellor.

Cromwell's interest switched to the splendid form and face of his fallen adversary. He smiled, triumphantly. Xusia might have been able to fool the rebels but he knew that inside this magnificent piece of sculpture made flesh dwelled the malevolent spirit of the ancient sorcerer himself. Xusia could assume a thousand different faces but he'd never hoodwink him!

"A fine, even superb duel, Xusia," he whispered in the ear of the sleeping giant. "In fact it was the finest I ever had. Pity we'll never learn who was the better. But I can't play games with you any more. You've caused me entirely too much mischief over the years. The time has come to set your earthbound soul free—and may it burn in Hades forever!"

Cromwell sprung to his feet, exhilarated by the tonic of believing he had Xusia in his lethal grasp at last. With the sorcerer once and for all out of his way—and after he eradicated the last remnant of the rebellion—nothing would stand in his path of becoming the ruler of the whole world!

"Bind him with fetters and chains and bleed him!" he yelled to his men, pointing to the still unconscious warrior. "I want no less than ten of you watching over this one at every moment. He is to be crucified at the feast tonight. It will be a show the kings will never forget!"

He strode across the courtyard toward a castle entrance, feeling prouder and younger than he had in years. He felt so potent, in fact, that he decided to visit the concubines before paying his respects to his bride-to-be, Alana.

The moment Cromwell disappeared around the corner a dozen Klaws began to jostle and vie with one another over ripping the steel gauntlet off the barbarian's hand. It would make a wonderful memento or trinket for one of their girls.

Seventeen

DARIUS WAS LYING UNDER a canopy of silks and perfumed veils, gazing out the unshuttered window. There was something about the round pink softness of the early morning sun that reminded him of Myra's lovely ass. Perhaps it was because the voluptuous whore's bottom was still practically staring him in the face—and because it had been the seat of so much pleasure for him these past twenty-four hours, ever since Talon had left on foot to tour the city of Elysium.

The thought of his beloved young leader pricked the bubble of his blissful contentment. He sat up in the bed of pillows and reached for his tunic and chain mail and began to dress.

The movement woke the sweet young whore—could she have been more than seventeen?—and she gazed up at him with the sad brown eyes of a doe and smiled gratitude; he had satisfied her too, many times. The girl had intelligence too, for she perceived he was now bemused and did not addle him with a lot of silly questions.

As Darius strapped his heavy sword around his hauberk he thought of the young man whom he had come to love as a younger brother. The mercenaries had agreed to meet Talon at midnight at the fountain in Elysium's huge public square. When he did not show up, they waited another hour and then returned to the bordello. They assumed he too was wenching somewhere and had forgotten the hour. Knowing them as well as he did the bordello would be the first place he would look for them. But by three A.M., when he still had not arrived, Ishmael volunteered to search for him, because of all the mercenaries he knew Elysium best.

Darius was pulling his boots on when the curtain separating his stall from the others flapped up and Ishmael hastily entered, his jowly red face the picture of sadness.

"Did you find him?" Darius asked, fearing the answer.

"Aye," the burly mercenary replied, glancing with no appetite at the bountifully built whore who was examining his bulk from head to toes. "But the king has him in chains."

Darius shot to his feet, tugging impatiently at the hilt of his sword. "Damn! What did he do? Have a go at one of Cromwell's favorite sluts?"

Ishmael lugubriously shook his massive head. "I fear that the offense is more grave than that, my friend. For they mean to execute Talon tonight—as part of the entertainment of the Feast of Kings."

"On my death they will!" Darius vehemently vowed. "We'll sink that plan quick enough!"

"But there's no way of getting to him, Darius! The castle is a veritable fortress and every entrance is securely guarded. We'll all perish if we try to storm the feast."

"Damn you, Ishmael! Then we all die! How many times has Talon risked his neck to save ours—or have you forgotten?"

"Of course I haven't, Darius. And don't be so self-righteous. I love him as much as you do. But we need more men than our handful of stalwarts—and I have no idea where to find them in time!" He threw up his hands in despair.

Once again the curtain was cast aside, this time admitting a squarely built, red-bearded man of forty-odd years. With a roguish grin and a wink, he said, "You've got your men, lads!"

Darius and Ishmael had forgotten that only curtains separated one stall from another and that the bordello was filled with customers besides them. They looked the stranger up and down, marked the red bandana tied around his head, the weatherbeaten features, the striped seaman's shirt over his barreled chest, and concluded he must be a pirate.

"Who are you?" Darius asked, "and why would you help our leader?"

"Me name's Morgan. I'll tell you why I'd gladly risk my ass and the hides of my men for your leader. Talon came to my rescue one night in a tavern when four mountain-size curs tried to slit my throat. Were it not for him I wouldn't be standing in front of you today."

Suddenly the possibility of saving their leader was no longer so remote. Their valor expanded with renewed hope.

"How many men do you have?" Darius pressed, the excitement of impending battle stirring his blood.

158

Before Morgan could reply one of his cohorts also entered the small stall. The whore hadn't had this many men in her stall since the night one of Cromwell's captains paid to watch her service two of his aides.

"We've only got twenty!" the new man said.

Morgan's enthusiasm at the prospect of a good fight and saving Talon wasn't about to be so easily deflated. "Aye, Eric, but as soon as we spread the word along the wharf that Talon's in trouble, I guarantee we'll have a hundred and more seadogs jump to rescue him. His exploits in the name of justice have won him friends in every port and city of Eh-Dan. And I personally know of at least a dozen men he's gotten out of a tough situation."

Morgan turned to Darius and Ishmael, beaming optimism. "No, lads, I assure you we'll have no trouble at all rounding up men for that hero. If nothing else the chance to give Cromwell the shaft will draw many." Then to Eric he abjured, "Now be off with you and get us an army!"

As Eric slipped under the curtain to do Morgan's bidding, the pillowy figure of the bordello's madam came into the stall, happily pulling Elizabeth, Cromwell's concubine, with her.

"Myra! Look at what the wind blew in!"

Darius, Ishmael and Morgan looked from the dumpy madam to the beautiful girl with lusty approval. Even in her long, loose blue robe her sinuous shape was impossible to conceal.

Myra jumped to her feet, ecstatic, totally indifferent to the fact that she was nude. The two girls embraced, tears of gladness streaking down Elizabeth's face.

"Elizabeth! How did you get free from that dreadful place! Oh, I've missed you so!"

"I was saved by the most gorgeous young man you've ever seen!" The words seemed to sparkle out of her pretty mouth. "You should have seen his chest and shoulders! And I could tell by the bulge under his tunic that his shaft was immense!"

At the mention of her rescuer the three men began to listen to the girls with serious attention.

"But why did he risk his life for you?"

"I really don't know, but he did. And he saved Mikah too—you know, the leader of the rebellion."

"Did this young man have a hand of steel, perchance?" Darius asked with unrestrained curiosity.

"Why, yes! How did you know?"

"He's our captain, that's why, you pretty wench!" He kissed her on the lips and slapped her playfully on her behind. "But, damn his beloved hide—now we must fetch him from your dog-king!"

"You mean—he's been captured?"

"Not only captured, peach blossom—but if Cromwell has his way Talon will be crucified tonight."

Elizabeth gasped, closing her tiny fists in anger. "No! He's too pretty! He's too good! He's too brave! We mustn't let that happen!"

"Precisely what we have in mind, sweet," Morgan interjected, aiming one of his roguish smiles at her.

Ishmael gently took one of her hands into his own. "You must know the layout of the castle as well as anyone."

Elizabeth smiled coyly. "Not only that—but I've

recently become acquainted with secret passages going in and out of the castle."

The three men exploded with cheers and rapturously encircled the two pretty girls with their arms, showering them with kisses, squeezing them and caressing them.

"Let's give Cromwell and his dogs," Darius exclaimed, "entertainment he'll never forget!"

Eighteen

IN THE EGG-SHAPED MIRROR ON a marble dressing table Alana studied her reflection, as the two slave girls brushed her long, loose dark hair and finished her makeup. The lids of her almond-shaped eyes were tinged with Nile green and outlined with charcoal black. The juice of the cherry stained her full lips the color of dark blood. And after hours of having her soft round shoulders and jutting breasts rubbed with ointments and creams they rode above her low-cut brocaded dressing gown smoother and creamier than she ever remembered them being.

In short, Alana never recalled looking more beautiful or, ironically, more unhappy. What was the point of resembling a radiant princess in a painting when the man who would benefit from it the most was also the man she most despised—while the man she now knew she loved was bound in chains and awaiting execution?

Word had circulated quickly of the young stalwart's capture, as well as the escape of her brother. And though her heart sang with joy at news of Mikah's freedom, the next second it quivered and cried when she learned of her new love's terrible fate.

Piling grief upon grief, as the late afternoon sun waned the black hour when Cromwell would force her to marry him drew nearer—with the even more repugnant hour approaching when the evil king would try to pluck her virgin's ruby, the very jewel she had hoped to present to the same gentle yet fierce giant below.

Cromwell burst into Alana's chambers without announcement, dismissing the slave girls with a brusque wave of his hand. He strode to her as if he already possessed her and stooped to plant a kiss on one of her bare shoulders. But Alana evaded the move by bolting upright and spinning out of his reach. He sneered. The rejection vexed but excited him too. He backed her into a corner from which she could not escape.

Alana's skin crawled. He looked at her as if she did not have the soft yellow gown on. And the thought of those steely hands and that cruel mouth ravishing her body made her want to retch.

Cromwell reached to pat her cheek and she recoiled again.

"Is that the way to treat your husband-to-be?" he mocked. The lecherous grin, narrowed eyes and curly tarnished gold hair made him look like an aging satyr.

Alana struggled with the urge to spit in his face. Then she marked the swelling bulge under his short white tunic and smiled. Why not? It could conceivably make him reevaluate whether he should risk bedding her.

Alana puckered her lips invitingly and pushed herself against him, slipping her fingers inside the top of his open tunic and toying with the swatch of hair on his chest. She even cooed a little.

Cromwell was at once tremendously aroused but cautious too. Was this some female wile?

"You're right, Titus. I've been stupid and ungrateful. What woman would not give her all to be your queen!" And with this outpouring of contriteness she began to grind her hips and tease his flexing shaft with the pressure of her silky womanhood. "Take me, my lord—now!"

Cromwell crushed her to his chest and began to rain kisses on her neck and shoulders, his hands gliding possessively over the lush curves of her body. He had just come from the concubines but the unexpected wantonness of this delicious beauty enflamed him once again. Perhaps she had weighed the advantages of being his queen and found them irresistible. Perhaps she had heard of his prowess as a lover from the slave girls and burned to ascertain it. Whatever the cause of her turnabout, she obviously lusted for him now—as he madly lusted for her!

As he attacked her like a ravenous wolf, Alana slowly worked one of her long legs between his and gently nestled it under his crotch, rubbing to stimulate him even more.

"After tonight . . ." he huskily said, between bites and kisses of her flesh, "you will be my queen! And soon you'll be the queen of the entire world! Oh, your mouth drips with honey! I will make love to you now as no other could!"

"With what!" she shouted into his ear, ramming her knee into his crotch.

Cromwell shrieked and staggered back, his face

white and twisted with agony. When the sharpest of the shooting pains subsided he began to slap and chase Alana about the vast chamber, holding his groin with one hand all the while. Equally as bad as the pain was the treacherous bitch's howling laughter and glowing contempt for him. Another clutch of pain stopped his pursuit and he leaned against the wall, glowering.

"Love me or not, you will be my queen—whore! And you will learn to beg me to stick my shaft into your sheath!"

"Ha! A cold day in hell that will be! Nothing will force me either to bed or to marry you!"

It was too humiliating to let this harlot see him doubled up with pain on the eve of their wedding night. And he would have her tonight even if he had to have her tied down in bed.

"Nothing, eh?" he snarled, limping toward the door. "Not even the life of your brother?"

Alana's heart stood still for a moment. Cromwell had touched the right button. For Mikah she would do anything—and she could tell by the sneer on Cromwell's face as he left her that he knew it too.

Nineteen

TO MEN WHO HAD SPENT their lives at sea or on horseback, being put in dungeons was more abhorrent than being flayed with barbed whips. Airless and sunless mousehole cells drive such men mad. And when such confinement is coupled with the smarting that comes from having had an important mission aborted, men in these situations are apt to turn on each other. Which is exactly what happened to Morgan and his pirates and Talon's mercenaries. It was not an hour after Cromwell's overwhelming numbers of Klaws had caught them raising an army and had thrown them into the castle's dungeons when these two factions began to rant and rave at one another—bandying accusations, blaming each other for their predicament and exchanging oaths and threats of retaliation.

Fortunately Cromwell's guards had seen fit to segregate the seamen and mercenaries in separate cells, otherwise they would have been at each others' throats.

"Whose idea was this blasted campaign!" Eric growled to no one in particular in the cell.

"It was these iron-brained landlubbers!" Morgan spat out between bars to the cell opposite them. "If we had taken another route—as I wanted to—and not waited for the slave girl to show us the way, we wouldn't be in these bloody roach- and rat-infested dungeons now!"

"Up yours!" Darius shouted from the mercenaries' cell. "And shut your yap or I'll wind these leg-chains around your scrawny neck!"

"If these gates weren't between us," Morgan flung back, "you'd be swimming in your own gizzards!"

All the men in both cells now rushed to the bars and began a relentless barrage of profanity and insults at each other. Soon they were throwing any object they could get their hands on across the walkway—tin plates and cups, broken stools, and even a few dead rats. In the midst of this volley of hurled objects and viturperation they rattled their cages unceasingly, the din reverberating through the gloomy, dank dungeons until Verdugo, the Royal Torturer, flung open the big iron door at the opposite end and came storming to their cells, where he stood shaking his clublike fists at the rioters.

"Shut up, vermin! Or I'll rip your tongues out!"

Now that the quarrelsome factions had a mutual and better enemy they transferred their spleen to him, vilifying him with every dirty word they could think of.

"Quiet, I said! I have a message for you from the king." He looked from one cell to the other. "Who's your leader?"

"I am," Darius spoke up.

167

Morgan had to bite his tongue to keep from challenging that assertion. But he was more interested in hearing what words the hairless bear had brought from the king than bickering any more with Darius.

"The king, in his boundless goodness, makes you a proposal. Tell us who sent you to invade the castle and he will show you mercy."

Darius' answer was to spit in Verdugo's face. The torturer thrust his bearish hands through the bars for Darius' throat but Darius stepped back in time. He proceeded to jeer and laugh at Cromwell's now anger-crazed henchman, as did the rest of the motley crew. Verdugo paced back and forth in front of the cells with his hands held out, opening and closing them, as if he were crushing eggs or skulls. "Laugh while you can, filthy pigs, for soon you will have no tongues at all!"

Verdugo turned to the two Klaws standing by the open door and beckoned them, a savage grin now cutting across his lardish face.

To their horror the prisoners watched the same guards drag into the dungeon two badly tortured but familiar figures—Ishmael and the slave girl Elizabeth. The men were too outraged by this pitiful sight to speak. Ishmael, his face battered to a pulp, was totally unconscious, while Elizabeth was only dimly aware of what was happening to her. One look at the area where blood had stained her robe was sufficient to tell she had been violated, God knew by how many men. And her pretty face was now swollen with purplish welts.

The guards deposited the victims directly in front of Morgan's cell. Elizabeth stretched her hand toward the cell for some loving human contact and Morgan reached through the bars and clasped it, his eyes filling with tears. The poor girl reminded him of his sister.

"No!" the seamen and mercenaries cried out in unison when Verdugo rested the tip of his sword on the small of the girl's back.

"Tell us who sent you," Verdugo screamed at the prisoners in general, "or the bitch dies here and now!"

Morgan never could stand seeing any woman suffer. And to have to witness this already half-dead girl suffer more pain was too much for him to bear. It was the need to save Talon's life that had inspired their rescue mission, not some mysterious person Verdugo kept referring to. But it was clear that if Verdugo did not get some positive response to his question the blade would pierce the dear girl's back. He was about to give Talon's name when Elizabeth, reading his purpose, laboriously lifted her head and, with the last ounce of her energy, shouted, "Tell him nothing! I am already dead!"

Before Morgan, Darius or anyone else could intercede Elizabeth pushed herself off the ground into Verdugo's sword, crying out like a little girl as the blade went through her back and out her stomach, the gleaming tip of the sword sticking out of her abdomen like a tiny diamond.

The girl's heroic sacrifice chilled the enraged mercenaries and seamen into a seething silence.

As Verdugo withdrew his blade from the girl's body Ishmael regained consciousness long enough to see what had happened and to make an ineffectual tackle for Verdugo's legs—just before the hairless lout rammed the sword right through the center of his face.

169

Verdugo sneered, pleased with his quick reflexes. But when he looked at the prisoners he was nearly knocked over by the intensity of their collective hate for him. He had the feeling that if he remained here another second the scorching hate in their eyes would burn the flesh off his bones.

Twenty

MACHELLI HAD JUST LEFT THE king in his private chambers and was on his way to the War Room, where Cromwell's chief generals waited for them. They would have to finalize the strategy for tonight without the king's presence. He had been in a foul mood and delegated Machelli to oversee the conference in his place.

"But, sire," he had implored the king, "they are your generals and, for such an important move, they would feel better if you personally sanctioned it. It is imperative that you preside over the conference!"

"It is imperative," Cromwell bellowed back, swinging away for a moment from the window he had been staring through into the spreading dusk, "that you obey my orders and stop questioning my will—*if* you wish to live! Now get out!"

Machelli retreated, bowing all the way out. He knew the reason for Cromwell's baleful state, for word of his ignominious encounter with Alana had already spread throughout the castle like wildfire. Actually he was delighted that the king had not deigned to attend the conference. With him representing the king's wishes he could make sure his own private designs would be executed.

The moment Machelli entered the vast beam-ceilinged room he sensed the restrained anarchy in the air. The three generals sitting at the huge round table did not like the plot Cromwell was cooking but they would stir it nevertheless because they were dutiful if dull soldiers. They gloried in conceiving stratagems for an honest battle. Trickery, court intrigue and the machinations of politics were alien to them.

Machelli took a seat at the head of the table. Except for the warm glow of a single lantern on the table the chamber was dark but alive with weaving shadows.

"Where's the king?" General Rumbolt grumbled. He was an unpolished man who had come up from the ranks and he was infamous for his bluntness and skill with a mailed fist.

"Pondering affairs of state. He has given me charge of the army until further notice."

The generals glowered with this news. They didn't like Machelli and made no bones at showing it. They looked upon him as an oily diplomat, not worth a candle beside a simple foot soldier.

"Let's get on with the report, Generals." There was no point on wasting the niceties of protocol on these uncouth louts. "What from you, General Thogan?"

The man in question had an ugly sword scar across his right cheek. "My knights will seal off the exits from the feast. No one will be able to get out."

Machelli turned to Rumbolt again. He was sitting to his right, heavy with thought. A man spends forty years shedding pints of blood for his country and he winds up taking orders from a slimy politician. "When the signal is given, my archers will kill every person at the feast."

Machelli looked to General Renquo to his left. The nervous tick under one eye was more fitful than ever. "You will see to it that all the bodyguards belonging to the kings and lords are dead a minute before the mass assassination begins.

General Renquo nodded.

Machelli addressed the three men collectively. "The instant Alana gives her vow to the king—kill everyone!"

The generals exchanged incredulous looks. As distasteful as Cromwell's gilded death-trap was to these more honest warriors, none could deny the scheme was dastardly clever. General Rumbolt was the first to break the silence that had enveloped them. And when he spoke, in spite of his personal bias against treachery of any kind, he was unable to keep the admiration for the audacity of Cromwell's plot out of his voice. "Imagine. All the nobility of Eh-Dan plus the kings of six great empires all wiped out in one fell swoop! There's no denying the king has genius of sorts."

"Which is why, gentlemen," Machelli exultantly proclaimed, "in three hours, Cromwell the King will be the most powerful man in the world!"

The three generals stared at the eelish chancellor, puzzled. Machelli's words glorified the king but somehow he made them sound as if he were really glorifying himself.

Twenty-One

THE EVENING WAS AS TRANSPARENT and sparkling as the waters of the blue lagoon. On a perfect evening like this under normal conditions the six kings assembled in the castle garden would have enjoyed taking a stroll along the flower-lined walkways, pausing perhaps to appraise the plethora of white and pink marble statues of voluptuous nymphs, leering satyrs, and gods and goddesses of Roman, Greek, Egyptian and Babylonian origin.

But the purpose of their imperial summons to the castle was so fraught with suspicion and doubt that it spoiled their appreciation of these truly resplendent grounds.

Dressed in their lavish tunics, capes and light armor beaten from precious metals, the six kings stood together before the garden fountain, its steady plume of water shooting a good ten feet high. Forming protective wings on either side of the solemn kings—but far back enough not to overhear their conversation—were the bodyguards,

174

dressed in the different colors of their respective nations.

"This treaty is worthless," said King Leonidas. He was spare of build, forceful in speech and known for his quick and invariably right decisions.

While Leonidas was dour by disposition, King Charles had a penchant for seeing some degree of humor in almost any situation. "If that be so, dear Leonidas, why have you chosen to leave your well-known harem girls to journey here?"

The kings laughed mildly.

"I believe the treaty to be worthless too," said King Ludwig, bringing them back to the gravity of the situation. "But I feel Cromwell will respect it so long as he has troubles within his own kingdom." He was as elegant in his demeanor as he was deadly with the sword.

"You are right," King Sancho grudgingly conceded. He was a man obsessed with having not only the last word but the first one too. "As long as Cromwell is faced with internal strife he cannot afford to alienate us. One day he might need us."

King Anthony, a boyish-looking man in his fifties, seldom had an original idea, and when he thought he had one he glowed with excitement in telling it. "I've got it! How about an alliance to crush Cromwell? If he's so weak now, it might be a good time to—"

The disapproval on Leonidas' face dropped Anthony's words in flight.

"Bah!" Leonidas jeered. "How many times have we tried to form alliances among ourselves and not kept them? Let's be honest, my lords, we

175

don't trust Cromwell but we don't trust each other either."

"But the fact that Cromwell combines his wedding with the signing of the treaty is a positive sign," King Louis interjected. "Surely the King would not stain his own wedding night with an act of treachery?"

"Taking that poor girl Alana to bed," King Charles quipped, "will be the biggest treachery of his life!"

The kings were still laughing when Louis pointed to a tall, rapier-thin figure swiftly moving towards them.

"Careful," the portly Louis admonished. "Here comes the snake Machelli!"

The chancellor gave this august body of men his most unctuous bow and made a grand sweep of his hand toward the courtyard entrance. "Your Royal Majesties—the feast begins! And what a sumptuous banquet of food and girls, plus an assortment of entertainments, the king has prepared for you!"

The six kings looked from one to the other and, in spite of their misgivings, they got behind the unfathomable Machelli.

"I've been waiting all day for this!" King Charles sarcastically quipped, evoking another round of mild laughter from the others. If Machelli heard this he acted as if he hadn't.

The castle courtyard had been appropriated for a gargantuan feast of food, drink, song and dance, in a twofold celebration of the royal wedding and the signing of the peace treaty. It was gaily decorated with multicolored banners, luxuriant sprays of flowers, burning urns of incense, barrels of wine and grog, dozens of blazing torches, and a raised dais upon which four musicians filled the limpid night air with the erotic melodies of flutes, a harp and an Italian lute.

With eighteen jaded and corrupt-looking lords and barons sprawled with their whores and wives around the main table—impatiently waiting for the arrival of the kings so they could attack the overflow of food and endless flasks and bowls of wine—plus half a dozen smaller tables where the less important knights sat with their mistresses and bugger-boys, the courtyard was bursting to maximum capacity. The laughter and ribaldry was continuous but there was an underlying restlessness for the feast to start.

The plaza was square of shape and encircled by two stories of the huge castle complex, with an entrance at each end and a massive oak door in the middle. It was through these doors that Machelli led the six kings, to the sudden blare of eight trumpeters announcing their arrival from a high balcony.

A roar of welcoming cheers went up from the guests as, to the joyous peals of the clarion trumpets, the kings marched to their special place at the head of the food-laden table. One of the first discordant notes they noticed in this festive atmosphere was the unfestive looking Black Klaws lining the second-floor balcony, which overlooked the feast and wedding area on the balcony below.

The second disquieting element in this flamboyant scene of opulence and jollity was the macabre centerpiece of the long, wide table to which Cromwell's puppet led them. Stripped to a mere dirty loincloth was a magnificently built young man in spreadeagle position, with iron stakes driven through his palms and his feet, tied to the table. His deeply tanned body and face were drenched in perspiration, as was his coal-black hair. Blood oozed from his ankles where the ropes cut in, as well as from his hands where the pinlike stakes were lodged. His soulful blue eyes blazed with pain and rage and, were not his mouth gagged with a steel plate, surely howls and shrieks of pain and denunciation would erupt from him so loud and horrific that the noise of the revelers would be diminished.

Once again the six kings exchanged looks of grim wonder. Was this poor wretched creature in the middle of the table, whomever he might be, Cromwell's perverse idea of entertainment?

The cheering and blare of the trumpets did not desist until the kings were seated at the table by fawning and scantily clad slave girls. "The whole thing smacks of an orgy—not a wedding and treaty celebration," King Charles whispered to King Ludwig.

Machelli excused himself on some pretext of conferring with the king again and left.

Now that the feast was officially launched the dissipated noblemen and painted ladies fell upon the cornucopia of food with the rapacity and indifference to etiquette of common peasants who hadn't eaten in weeks. The fact that they often had to reach across the young giant's pilloried body to grab for the platters of roast pig, duck and beef did not seem to lessen their appetites one whit. On the contrary, the unbridled sensualists appeared to derive fiendish pleasure every time they dripped juices and gravies on his body in helping themselves.

To add to the pathetic captive's humiliation the

celebrants laughed and poked fun at him, occasionally spitting undigested morsels of food on his mammoth chest. Flushed with wine, the women and homosexuals at the table were the worst offenders, for they would joke about the size of the man's organ, which was so clearly defined through his rags. Some of the bolder wenches reached over and groped his member or pinched one of the nipples of his swollen pectorals.

Fully engrossed now in satiating themselves with food and drink, the kings huddled as close together as the table permitted to discuss the identity and purpose of having the crucified young man at what was supposed to be a joyous occasion. King Leonidas had been eyeing the captive with the most scrutiny. He had not been able to either eat or drink in the light of the young man's agony. Slowly he realized he recognized him.

"My God!" he declared under his breath, tilting toward King Ludwig. "Isn't that Talon—the leader of a band of mercenaries? I once had secret cause to use him and his men."

Ludwig's eyes narrowed on the pilloried giant, "I did too, Leonidas. Hmmm. He certainly is big enough to be Talon. But I seem to remember some kind of a steel gauntlet on one of his hands."

The other kings had similar experiences with Talon. They liked him. He had been as brave as he was fair about the fee he exacted for his mercenaries. What's more, on several occasions he had done favors for them and had not charged a talent. Talon and his men had always been a good emergency squad to hold in reserve.

Leonidas rose off his pillow and whispered to

the others, "I must get a closer look to be sure it's him."

The guests were so busy swilling wine and gorging food that no one paid attention to the spare king threading his way through the milling guests to the spreadeagled young man. When he was directly behind the head of the prisoner he looked deep into his eyes. There was no mistaking those singularly blue orbs or the unique combination of princely gentleness and savagery on those chiseled features. The light of recognition also seemed to beam in Talon's eyes. And the longer he studied Talon's pain-racked face the more furious the king became. To have done anything as vile as crucifying this selfless and noble free spirit was the epitome of inequities! He couldn't and wouldn't stand by and let Cromwell maim another inch of the good mercenary. When he thought no one was looking, Leonidas bent forward and whispered in Talon's ear, "Have courage! You are not without friends here!"

He returned to the table. "It's him!" he said, sotto voce.

For the first time in their dealings with one another the kings were unified by a common bond of anger.

"Every one of us here owes Talon a favor," Leonidas resumed. "We can't let him die like a dog!"

"What are you proposing?" asked King Charles.

"That at the right moment we call in our own guards, free Talon, climb our mounts and ride out of here with him. Possibly during the marriage ceremony. By then most of these reprobates," he pointed to the revelers, "will be too drunk to fight, and Cromwell will be so dreamy with thoughts of

180

his nuptial bed that no one will have a full head to stop us."

"But the treaty!" Ludwig protested.

"Come on!" King Charles jeered, now clearly throwing his lot in with Leonidas. "You know deep down, as every one of us at this table knows, that the treaty is a farce."

King Anthony nodded. "Cromwell has something up his sleeve. I know it."

Noting some reluctance still in King Sancho and King Louis, Leonidas looked them in the eye and firmly said, "If I have to I'll free Talon alone! Without going into embarrassing detail—I literally owe that young man my life, and maybe even my kingdom."

"It means war with Cromwell if we interfere," Ludwig warned, but tilting toward Leonidas' side.

"It would mean war with him sooner or later anyway. How say you all, Lords? Are you with me?"

"Aye!" the kings whispered in unison.

Twenty-Two

THE AGONY OF HIS SPIKED hand was excruciating. But the soul-pain he felt watching the ceremony unfold on the balcony was worse.

Trumpets blared a bridal march and the coarse merriment surrounding him seemed to accompany the brassy joyous music. But to Talon he was listening to an abysmally depressing dirge. For if the abominable marriage between Cromwell and Alana did take place—and unless a miracle happened it certainly would—for him it would be a death of sorts. The corpse was a dream he now realized he had carried in his chest since the first day he laid eyes on Alana as a boy, which was to one day marry her himself. If only he could spit out the gag and scream and howl like a wolf for its lost mate he'd feel some degree of relief. But the steel plate seemed permanently locked over his mouth, as did the spikes through his throbbing palms.

He looked up once more at the ornately decorated atrium on the balcony, where a priest in flowing white robes had just arrived and acknowledged with a perfunctory smile the twelve beautiful bridesmaids waiting for the king and Alana. Like another spike driven through him—this time through his heart—he saw a sad but oh so lovely Alana emerge from a balcony wing, accompanied by two more bridesmaids. She was absolutely beautiful and ravishingly virginal in her tightly clinging white silks. But as radiant a vision as she projected, Talon could tell, even from where he was nailed to the table, that Alana was miserable through and through. Like a mourner at a funeral instead of a woman about to become a bride, Alana looked neither left or right, nor raised her lambent brown eyes, nor cast so much as a glance at the frolicking guests below in the courtyard, who were now settling into respectful silence. Throughout these proceedings she was as if mesmerized.

Alana's wretchedness was Talon's torment. He could endure his own suffering easier than hers. He began to frantically pull on the spikes, but the augmented pain incurred therewith was too great and he had to stop. Then Cromwell's abrupt appearance from the opposite wing sent searing bolts of anger through his brutalized body again. Cromwell was dressed in a silken mantle of white with gold trimming along the edges. A red velvet cape flowed down from his squared shoulders. Atop his head was the royal crown encrusted with rubies and diamonds. His strong jaw was imperiously thrust upward and he was so obviously and smugly pleased with himself that Talon wanted to retch.

Talon went mad with frustration. Once more he bucked and tugged at the vicious spikes and cutting ropes like a wild horse trussed on the ground. But neither the ropes nor the spikes gave an inch. Still he struggled to break free. Nothing mattered to him but preventing that discordant pairing from taking place, neither his pain, the Cause, Mikah nor his own life. He'd sacrifice everything to save Alana from the concupiscent coils of Cromwell's rampant lust.

"Join hands and kneel my children!"

The priest's words echoed down to Talon from the balcony.

The king had to seize Alana's limp hand by her side, holding it tightly in case she tried to pull away. Still her head hung despairingly low and she seemed oblivious to her surroundings. Cromwell now made her kneel beside him.

And now the short, epicene priest began to make religious signs over the crestfallen bride and triumphant king, while he recited marriage vows in a hybrid Latin.

"*Prodeas, nova nupta, si. Iam videtur, et audias. Et beata viri tui, quae tibi sine serviat . . .*"

The guests nearest to the fettered young giant began to wonder if perchance epilepsy—the disease of the gods—had not entered his body, for his fists continually clenched convulsively on the spike heads, while he tossed his handsome head from side to side, seemingly indifferent to the pain these twistings and paroxysms were causing him.

Unbeknown to anyone at this lavish fête, save the king and a select few, while the priest chanted his litany, in another part of the castle General Rumbolt's archers dipped their arrows in a cauldron of poison. When they were finished, they surreptitiously entered the castle and replaced the regular guards on the second balcony. The celebrants below were too engrossed with the marriage ceremony to notice the archers slipping arrows into their bow strings.

General Thogan's men were also busy, their job being to seal off all the courtyard exits.

In the pretty castle gardens, where earlier the six kings had conferred, a squad of General Renquo's soldiers stealthily surrounded the six kings' bodyguards and, with one fell swoop, killed them with daggers, swords and spears.

These three separate but interrelated moves spelled turning the courtyard into a deathtrap for the kings inside.

Ever since the guards had dragged the horribly mutilated bodies of Elizabeth and Ishmael away from their sight the mercenaries and pirates had been sunk in prickly gloom. From the remarks overheard between Verdugo and the guards they knew about the wedding taking place upstairs and Talon's cruel predicament. And as these atrocities went on unchecked, the raiders stewed in helpless frustration, awaiting either Verdugo's instruments of torture, the arrow or the guillotine. To die fighting was an honorable death. But to die like sheep led to the slaughter was to compound death with shame.

"What's that?" Darius asked, jumping to the bars.

In the opposite cell Morgan and his buccaneers also rushed to the bars and strained to see who was coming into their cell block.

When the iron door flew open and three fiery, beautiful concubines from Cromwell's harem came sprinting to their cells, they couldn't believe their eyes. The men gasped and made excla-

185

mations of disbelief. Were these transparently clad girls lovely apparitions manufactured by the fever of their frustrations?

The spunkier of the three concubines—with hair like spun gold and lascivious green cat's eyes—carried a huge ring of keys. While she looked over the men in both cells her saucy companions kept warily glancing at the door.

"Where are the men who came to save the good-looking warrior with the hand of steel?"

"We are!" the men in both cells shouted back.

"All right. Listen carefully. We haven't too much time." Her soft voice was sparked with anger. "We know what happened to our beloved sister Elizabeth—and we want to make Cromwell pay for it! And we know that the best way to get the king is to spoil his wedding and the horrible game he plays with your friend upstairs!"

"What's your name, little spitfire?" Morgan asked, impressed by the pretty woman's pluck.

"Bar-Bro. But that's not important. Your friend can be killed at any moment. We must act at once if we are to save him!"

"Open these doors, sweet angel," Darius urged, "and you'll have your revenge!"

The mercenaries and pirates roared their unanimous support.

Bar-Bro quickly unlocked the cells and the warriors came pouring out, itching to get their hands on weapons. She tossed the ring of keys to the good-looking tough who had promised her revenge. "Here. The armory is on the other side of the door."

As the raiders tore down the walkway Darius lingered with Bar-Bro long enough to say, "When all this is over I'd like to show you a mercenary's idea of fun!"

She smiled encouragingly and playfully pushed him towards the others.

In the dungeon armory they grabbed every weapon in sight. Armed to the teeth with swords, daggers, maces and spears, the men let their lovely liberators lead them through the maze of dungeons. But as they were about to file past the Torture Chamber they couldn't resist settling one score.

Verdugo was in the act of sharpening an assortment of blades on his huge stone wheel when he found himself suddenly besieged on all sides by a myriad of flashing knives. Through the shock of multitudinous stabs all over his rocky body, just before the light left his shifty eyes forever he heard a tiny sweet voice whisper, "This is for Elizabeth, pig!"

". . . uxor, vivamus it viximus, et teneamus . . ."

A silky movement from the balcony on the second floor distracted Talon from the priest's cryptic words. When he looked up a shudder went through his tortured body. Cromwell's archers were raising their bows and taking aim at the kings below. My God, what kind of a beast was Cromwell? Who but an irredeemable fiend would think of mixing his wedding ceremony with the spilling of his supposed guests' blood! If the miracle, or King Leonidas, or an upsurge of superhuman strength did not spring his fetters in the next couple of minutes, not only would Alana be married to the man who had butchered his family, but the lives of six noble kings would be snuffed out.

187

Using the appalling sight of Alana being co-erced into a loathsome marriage as a maddening spur, Talon drew upon his last reservoir of strength to pull on the stakes again, the tension causing another spillage of blood. He tugged and used his chest, shoulders and arms to bring lever-age on the iron pins. He found himself watching the marriage ceremony through a blinding white-hot haze of pain—but still he fought off passing out and redoubled his Herculean effort to break free. Like salt rubbed into open wounds, he continued to use the priest's chanting words to lash himself onward.

"Do you, Titus Cromwell, Lord God on earth, King of Eh-Dan, take this woman to be your bride, your queen and mother of your children?"

Mother of Cromwell's children! Talon held fast to that repellant image as yet another spur, and it was then that he thought he sensed one of the spikes budge.

"I do!" Cromwell's voice proudly boomed across the courtyard, to the delight of the celebrants—ex-cepting of course the kings and the young man engaged in a titanic life and death struggle on the table.

"Then repeat after me," the priest droned on. *"Quando tu Alana, ego Titus..."*

Talon's swollen muscles were strained and quivering to the breaking point. They knotted and stretched like iron cables, as he worked the spikes back and forth, both in his hands and the wood beneath them. He had been so long encased in dire pain that he seemed numb to it now. Only when he allowed himself to focus on the shooting shards of pain did the numbness cease, and when that happened he longed to scream his head off.

188

"Do you, Alana, daughter of Lord Duncan, take this man to be your groom, your—"

The dreaded words lashed his nerves into a final frenzy of effort. It was now or never. Nor could he allow himself to be distracted by the number of guests who had become aware of his struggle and were moving away from the table, wondering whether to call the guards or to ignore him. Slowly, as if tearing up the deep roots of a tree, the spikes began to give. And as he finally tore loose from the wood in a primal burst of energy he experienced a flashing kaleidoscope of different impressions; the Klaw archers readying to fire, King Leonidas rising and drawing his sword to help him, and the priest asking, "Do you take this man to be your husband?"

All within a matter of seconds, Talon sprung forward, pulled the spikes out of his hands and flung them at the revelers, ripped away the gag and yelled, before Alana could answer the priest's question, *"Cromwell!"* It was the blood-curdling cry of a wild beast breaking loose from his cage, a cry of vengeance as well as liberation.

Pandemonium instantly broke loose in the packed courtyard and on the balconies. Alana rushed to the balcony's edge and gazed helplessly at Talon struggling to unbind his feet, as a storm of noblemen bore down on him with swinging swords. But a raging Cromwell whipped his arms about her tiny waist from behind and dragged her through a wing of the balcony before she could see his attackers suddenly deflected by the six kings with their own swords drawn.

Added to the expanding chaos was the shrieking and sword-swinging tumult of Talon's mercenaries rushing into the courtyard from one end, and Morgan's pirates charging in from the other. Already covered with the blood of the Klaws they cut down outside, the raiders now unleashed their pent-up frustrations and rage at the surprised knights, lords and inrushing Klaws with the smashing suddenness of a typhoon—and they rapidly went down under the storm of the raiders' blades in a sea of their own spurting and gushing blood.

When King Leonidas saw that Talon could not get free of the ropes without a blade, he jumped up on the table and cut the binding with one slice. Before Talon could spring to his feet, he caught sight of the archers readying to release a volley of arrows at his friends and mercenaries. He was about to shout, "Look out!" when he saw Mikah, Rodrigo and the other rebels pouring onto the balcony to fall upon the archers. Talon sprung to his feet and ached to join them in the fray that ensued, and he wildly looked around for a sword.

"Talon!" he heard his beloved Darius shout. He turned in his lieutenant's direction. There, standing also on the long table not twenty feet away, was Darius grinning and warding off a Klaw with one sword and holding Talon's tri-bladed sword in the other hand. "Here!" he shouted again, tossing Talon's sword at him. "Join the fun!"

Talon caught the tri-bladed sword by the hilt and instantly felt a surge of power infuse him. The weapon was more than just an ingeniously designed sword. It was a symbolic blood-tie with his father, King Richard. And when he had its long contoured hilt in his hand, he felt that the martial spirit of his father was also wielding the sword with him. Oddly enough, now that he was holding the gift that Richard had given him on the eve of his murder, he felt no pain surrounding the drying punctures through his palms.

Talon spiritedly spun around three times on the table like a whirling dervish, wildly swinging the tri-bladed sword over his head and howling a battle-cry of such volume and piercing decibels that it was heard above the screams of the fleeing women and dying soldiers.

He now sped like a marathon runner down the table—lopping any Klaws' heads that he passed in progress—and made a flying leap for the long velvet drapes hanging on steel rings from the three-storied overhang. He grabbed hold of the thick material and used the momentum he had generated running to swing with the drape to the balcony where Mikah and his rebels were fiercely engaged in battle. At once he savagely plunged into the siege, felling one Klaw after another. Side by side he fought with Mikah and Rodrigo, exhorting them to greater and greater ferocity, himself shearing and hacking through the Klaws with dauntless vigor.

When he perceived that Mikah's rebels could more than handle the Klaws' dwindling ranks up here, Talon shouted above the fray, "I'm off to retrieve your sister and ax Cromwell!"

He leaped and rode the drapes again, this time to the courtyard, where he bounded over tables and sundered bodies to the nearest exit. But he stopped cold when he ran head-on into a Klaw wearing the steel gauntlet he had stolen from his hand. Talon howled with outrage and with one swift unerring swipe he lopped the Klaw's hand bearing the steel brace. Ignoring the screams of the offender, Talon stepped over his convulsing body to the severed hand, ripped away the gauntlet and slipped it back on his own left hand, where it had been for many years. Feeling secure because his trademark was once again on his person, Talon shouldered and cut his way through three more Klaws and plunged outside into the night.

Twenty-Three

CONNECTING ONE WING OF THE castle
with another was a long, wide, pillared arcade
with a high, vaulted ceiling and green frescoed
walls. Because of its hollow interior the slightest
sound carried like a pebble dropped in a deep
well. The long, slanting shadows cast by the flaming wall torches on the tiled floors and spaces between the pillars created a forestlike effect.

Hurrying through these thickets of shadows
and stone pillars like hunters fleeing with a
poached quarry were Cromwell and five Black
Klaws. Slung over one of Cromwell's shoulders
was a trussed and gagged Alana.

The king's head still whirled with the unbelievable events that had occurred in the courtyard.
How was it possible that everything he had
planned with such flawless precision went so
wrong so fast? Rebels invading the castle through
secret passages, mercenaries and sea scum mysteriously escaping from the dungeons, the kings
turning on him, the ruining of the marriage cere-

mony, and the so-called leader of the mercenaries pulling free of three-inch stakes by sheer brute strength and will power!

Cromwell sneered. Everything went wrong because supernatural forces were once more at play against him, as they had been from the cursed day he had mistakenly resurrected the sorcerer. In other words, once more the diabolical handwork of Xusia was evident in the destruction of his plans. And more than ever he was convinced that Xusia's evil spirit resided in the godlike body of that young hulk. Who else but a sorcerer of extraordinary powers could have torn loose from his own pilloring?

Without turning around the king recognized the light steps of Machelli running to catch up with him.

"Excellency! Wait!"

Cromwell slowed down until his worrisome chancellor was at his side.

"Fearing some kind of chicanery on the kings' part," Machelli blurted out, "I put the army on the alert several days ago. They are gathered at this very moment high in the mountains waiting for your appearance."

Cromwell smacked Alana's behind because she began to kick and squirm over his shoulder. Then he looked at Machelli with a suspicious eye. "Quite perceptive of you to assume something might go wrong." He made no attempt to conceal the sarcasm.

"I'm always looking out for your majesty. With you at the head of the full force of your army, you will once and for all crush this puny but annoying rebellion."

"Not so puny," Cromwell's angry voice boomed

in the arcade, "if you remember what happened back there in the courtyard!"

Suddenly the demon he had tried to crucify tonight stepped out from behind a pillar, blocking the procession.

"You have a big voice, Cromwell. Pity you haven't got the courage to match it."

Cromwell stared at his antagonist, incredulous. Where did he materialize from? He was still only partially clad and his shoulders, arms and massive chest were splotched with fresh blood. In his steeled hand he held a deadly looking three-bladed sword. It was Xusia himself—as he wished he could look like all the time.

"How did you get from the courtyard to here so fast?" He was sure that someone in his own court was in league with the wizard.

"A sweet old gentleman by the name of Devereux whispered the castle's secrets in my ear."

Devereux! He should have guillotined that senile fart years ago! And he would have liked to wipe that supercilious smile off the audacious upstart's face permanently! On his life he would make this young peacock crow for mercy!

"Here, Machelli. Take her!" He transferred the burden of Alana into his arms, motioned the Klaws to hold back and then unsheathed his sword. "Wait here with the baggage, Machelli. This shouldn't take long."

Cromwell began to cockily circle his adversary. He had been recapitulating their last clash over and over again since it happened, and he was positive he now knew the young giant's weak points with the sword. "This time, Xusia—and don't pretend you're somebody else—you will die!"

195

Once more Talon wondered who this mysterious Xusia might be.

For the second time in forty-eight hours Talon's and Cromwell's swords made sparks in the dark, the clash of their heavy blades resounding throughout the arcade.

While the king and his opponent crossed swords, swearing at each other with each thrust and whack, Machelli seized the opportunity to slip behind a huge pillar and, out of sight and earshot of the Klaws, he propped Alana against the pillar and quickly untied her.

She sighed with relief and rubbed her sore wrists and ankles, studying Machelli with a mixture of gratitude and confusion. "Then you really are on our side?"

"Of course, my lady. I always have been."

"For a while I couldn't tell."

They both spoke in hushed tones.

"Come, Alana. We must get you to safety."

"Where?"

"To the catacombs under this very castle, and which no one knows about save a very select few. The catacombs will lead us to a boat I have waiting for us at Fisherman's Cove."

"But what about him," she asked, pointing to Talon, "and Mikah?"

He patted her hands reassuringly. "That one will take care of himself, I assure you. As for your brother, he waits for us in the very same boat! Come!"

He took her by the hand and led her around the tall, stout pillars without arousing the duelists' or the Klaws' attention. They would have disappeared from the arcade unnoticed but for the bursting open of a door at the opposite end of the arcade, through which Mikah and the rebels came storming into the scene.

The intrusion for a moment stopped the puffing and sweating swordsmen.

The Klaws pulled on their swords.

Alana jerked her hand out of Machelli's. Mikah? But Machelli had said he was at—? Why had he lied to her? She started to back away from him, just as the Klaws clashed swords with the rebels and the king and Talon resumed dueling. "You're not on our side, are you—theirs or ours? You have some kind of nefarious scheme of your own, don't you! Stay away from me!"

Machelli smacked her across the face, threw her screaming and kicking over his shoulder and raced out with her the way he came.

Cromwell did not miss this development. Machelli was running off with his future queen! Stopping and punishing the treacherous swine was of more importance than slicing the sorcerer in disguise. "Finish him off for me!" he yelled to his men. Two Klaws instantly took his place fighting the fierce warrior. "Dismember him and throw the pieces to the dogs!" He tore off after Machelli and his stolen prize, Alana.

"Take my place, Mikah!" Talon shouted. "I'm going after Alana before Cromwell gets her again!"

"Go, good friend! We will soon follow!"

As Mikah and his twelve men vanquished the five Klaws in rapid order, Talon streaked around the pillars and tried to catch up with the king.

Twenty-Four

THE CASTLE HAD BEEN UNWITTINGLY built on top of a network of catacombs. Once persecuted religious sects conducted their forbidden ceremonies here. Later, the secret witches of Elysium performed pagan rites here, which involved crossbreeding snakes of different species. Naturally phosphorescent minerals and cracks of light from above the catacombs bathed them with an unearthly luminosity night and day. And creeping through these corkscrew shafts of greenish radiance were underground streams and stagnant pools.

Neither the reptiles that had been spawned here nor the profusion of shafts bothered Machelli. He was at home here. Because he was attuned to the reptilian mind the snakes left him alone. He flourished in the shadowy world of the catacombs. It suited his personality and values well.

He was holding his hand over Alana's mouth, pressed into a deep niche in the cavern wall as

Cromwell sprinted past them with the look of a mad dog on his face. He was full of malicious glee knowing the frustrated king was running into a maze of shafts in which he would probably get lost. And as he continued to hold Alana from behind, her silky round buttocks pressing against his crotch were beginning to arouse him. But he would postpone gratifying awakened desire until he had her alone in the secret cavern chamber he had appropriated for himself in the catacombs.

Machelli was about to remove his hand from Alana's soft mouth when he heard the more thunderous gait of the young giant pounding toward them. He tucked himself and his prisoner more tightly into the niche until the new runner shot past them too, hot on Cromwell's trail. When Machelli thought it was safe, he jumped out of the niche with Alana and, his powerful hand still over her mouth, he dragged her in the opposite direction from the one Talon and Cromwell had taken.

Once Machelli had slammed the round wooden door shut, the full realization of being absolutely alone with him hit Alana with the impact of a fist. What was she doing here? His purpose of absconding with her escaped her. Nor did she have any insight regarding why he had been obviously two-facing Mikah and the king.

The sight of a giant pink and white speckled iguana lounging on a quartz rock did not make her feel any more secure. And when she saw the half-submerged monstrous serpent eyeing her from a shallow stream of turbid water running through the torchlit chamber, she instinctively sprung forward, unwittingly making herself prey

199

to Machelli's outstretched arms, which were, considering how slender he was, like iron rods encircling her. Alana tried to break free but she couldn't.

For the first time since he had abducted her, Alana had a chance of observing his face at close range. His normally swarthy complexion now seemed pasty and there was almost a reptilian cast to the way his heavily hooded eyes unwaveringly stared at her. Strange. She had never noticed the unpleasant shape of his eyes before.

"What now?" she asked with forced flippancy, in an effort not to let him see how terrified she was.

Machelli released one of his hands from her back to point a finger at himself. "This door leads to power, Alana! You can be part of it—or a victim of it. In other words, my desirable wench, I invite you to become my lady!"

With this totally surprising proposal to her Machelli pressed his thick cold lips on her neck while pushing his rigid member against her. She was as appalled as she was bewildered. First her beloved rescuer tried to seduce her, next the king tried to rape her, and now Machelli! What was there about her that made men think she would spread her legs the moment they expressed desire for her? The anger at such demeaning presumption overrode her fear of Machelli. Though it could conceivably cost her her life she felt compelled to teach the now panting chancellor a lesson. The lesson she had in mind had worked twice before, and why not a third time?

"Power excites me so!" she moaned, relaxing now wholly into his arms.

Machelli's ego responded exactly as she had expected it to. He was smacking his lips and smirking, utterly convinced his charm had stirred her.

She adopted her most seductive voice. "Without your help Mikah's rebellion would never have gotten off the ground. And to a woman, Machelli, power and cunning are the most potent of aphrodisiacs—and you are both incarnate! I've always lusted for you from afar! Whatever your cause—take me with you!"

Disgustedly, Alana could feel his member straining to burst through his cockpiece.

"You are wiser than your tender years, Alana."

She bit him gently on the neck and then blew hot breaths into his ears, all the while subtly positioning her knee under his crotch.

Machelli started to unfasten the back of her temptingly revealing wedding gown. Through the material his shaft was poised. "You will promise to obey my every wish—in and out of bed?"

"Oh, yes, master!" Alana ecstatically moaned. "But you must obey *this*!" She plowed her knee into his balls as hard as she could. But instead of screaming out with pain—as any normal man would have done—Machelli did not so much as wince. Terror gripped every fiber of her being. If Machelli's responses were not normal human responses—then what in God's name kind of creature was he?

He continued to clutch her in his arms a moment longer, sneering. So the bitch had been playing with him. Well, if she was not aroused by the swarthy form of Machelli, perhaps she'd warm better to his real visage.

A low, inhuman growl emerged from the bowels of his being, and he hurled her against a natural stone pillar that protruded from the wall on the other side of the chamber. When Alana recovered from the impact of the throw she found herself riveted to the pillar with invisible bolts that seemed to emanate from Machelli.

Slowly, with a studied solemnity and evil grandeur, he took long, measured strides toward her and began speaking in a low, raspy subhuman voice that she never heard before.

"Your brother botched the plans I had woven for Cromwell with such infinite care. But I will not let you, my saucy virgin, get away with botching the plans I had in mind for you!"

Still stuck to the pillar like steel shavings to a magnet, Alana watched Machelli approach her with horrifying disbelief. Before her very eyes she was witnessing a transformation that was as hideous as it was mindboggling. First the alteration of voice and now his very features grew fluid and rearranged themselves, twisting, stretching and reshaping. Where there were once teeth there were now fangs. Skin that had been human became leathery, yellow, reptilian. And his limbs under the black tunic were suddenly so loose of movement she would not have been surprised to discover his body hung on coils rather than bones. She was simultaneously repulsed and fascinated by the grotesque creature Machelli had become. His bulbous head and serpent's face were now only inches from her own.

"See me, Alana, as I truly am . . ." He rested a scaly hand on her bare shoulders and she shivered with disgust. She started to scream at the top of her lungs, still magnetized to the pillar. Her screams seemed to please him and he smiled, exposing the teeth of a saber-tooth tiger or wolf.

"You could have been my queen, stupid girl. My sow to ravish and give unheard of pleasure to. But your treachery will make you my victim instead!"

He tilted his mouth to sink his teeth into the soft whiteness of her throat when the door suddenly burst open and Cromwell charged into the chamber, slashing at the air like a maniac.

One look at the familiarly slimy creature wearing Machelli's clothes told him at once his colossal mistake. It was not the form of the steel-handed warrior that housed the sorcerer's spirit—but Machelli's! He felt like dashing his head against the walls. Stupid ass that I am, he silently ranted at himself. "Xusia! So it's Machelli's body in which you've been hiding these many years!"

Xusia laughed from the bottom of his throat.

Alana remained hanging from the pillar, limp and speechless from the grotesque wonders she had seen.

To have had killing access to Xusia so easily in Machelli's form, and not know it, was a scalding humiliation that he could not brook another second. He released a drawn-out hiss of total hate and lunged for Xusia with the accumulated fury of eleven years of frustration.

But though Xusia was swordless and standing directly in line with the thrust of Cromwell's sword, instead of slicing through the sorcerer's gelatinous shape, his blade hit and bounced off a field force surrounding Xusia that was like an invisible wall of stone. "Ahhhh!" he shrieked, rubbing his sprained wrist. When he glanced from Alana's look of total shock to Xusia again—marking those malevolent eyes burning like hot red coals—

he suddenly remembered what had happened to the witch Ban-Urlu on Tomb Island so long ago. He began to quake with fear. Was he too to suffer her horrible fate? He would not wait to find out. He dashed for the smashed open door. But even as he ran Xusia started chanting demonic affirmations that resulted in Cromwell being lifted off the ground by a giant unseen hand and pitched to the slippery stones, where he was forced to lie, again, as if an invisible hand or weight held him down.

"My body is a temple wherein all demons dwell!" Xusia droned, shuffling toward the prostrate king.

"A pantheon of many souls and demons under one flesh am I!" As he inched closer and closer to the king his eyes bulged with stark terror. When the sorcerer lifted and pointed one of his power-charged hands at Cromwell he began to froth at the mouth because he knew the end was near.

"The time has come for the world to be rid of your vileness, Cromwell—for there can only be one Lord of the Universe, and that one is *me*—not you!"

Cromwell's gums began to bleed and blood leaked out of his nose and ears.

Xusia was too busy enjoying Cromwell's suffering and the king was too much in agony for either of them to notice the thirty-foot snake slithering out of the turbid water and creeping toward Alana. Try as she could, Alana could not release the screams locked in her constricted throat. In the silent paralysis of terror she watched and then felt the serpent's langorous, almost amorous body coil around her own. And when its bulbous head weaved and bobbed in front of her face—its forked tongue darting in and out of its ruby-red mouth—she fainted.

"Eleven years ago, Cromwell," Xusia rasped, in funeral tones, "you stuck your blade in this sorcerer's flesh and assumed him to be dead! But it takes more than cold steel to slay a real sorcerer, you fool—and now you will die a death that only a sorcerer can provide!"

"Spare me!" Cromwell pleaded for his life. But Xusia ignored his cries and knelt beside him. He raised his taloned fingers over the king's chest and, without so much as touching him, demonic energy poured from his fingers, and the brittle bones of Cromwell's chest cavity began to bend and crack. The king screamed in sheer agony as he vainly tried to rear himself up off the floor.

His bones would have fatally cracked had not Talon come charging into the chamber, wielding his mighty tri-bladed sword. His sudden appearance deflected Xusia from the slow, bizarre, agonizing murder of Cromwell.

One absorptive sweep with Talon's eyes registered the situation in the chamber. There was Cromwell with a fiend that could only be the Xusia he kept confusing him with. They were surprised and vulnerable to a swift attack. But, horror of horrors, there was also Alana wrapped in the contracting coils of a monster serpent, as it carried his sweet darling into the turbid stream. There was no second thought regarding what task he had to accomplish first.

Talon raced past Xusia and the prostrate king when the sorcerer bolted to his feet and blocked his way.

"Move, dog!" Talon shouted. "I have no quarrel with you!"

But Xusia bobbed left and right in front of Talon every time he tried to go around him.

Talon had no time to play games. He hoisted his sword high above the sorcerer's head and brought it down with a force that could have split a rock in two. But the same thing happened to him that did to Cromwell; his blades came up against an invisible shield protecting Xusia and the sword bounced back in painful recoil.

"Stay put, mercenary!" Xusia rasped, his reddish orbs gleaming daggers. "The sow Alana is mine—not yours!"

"Now we do have a quarrel!" Talon roared in Xusia's face, while helplessly watching the snake slide out of the water with Alana tied to its tail, as it crawled into a dark cave within the chamber.

Once again Talon tried to hack his way through the unseen shield protecting Xusia and again his sword recoiled so high that he nearly severed his own head. Before he could swing again or tackle Xusia with his bare hands, the sorcerer drove Talon down on his knees with supernatural mind-power, holding him on his knees without any physical contact whatsoever. Talon used his own willpower and concentration of energies to repel Xusia's mantric forces—but he was only human, while Xusia was half-man, half-demon and a wizard to boot.

"Thou dost loll alone in wanton sloth and crimson halls of dissipation!" Xusia once again droned, while he manipulated occult powers.

The words made no sense to him. But with each word Talon felt his life's sap being sucked out of him a little more, as if Xusia had fastened a vampire bat to his jugular vein. And when he experienced the sensation of blood seeping out of his gums, ears and nose—as it was for Cromwell lying petrified beside him—Talon realized he might very well die ignominiously in these macabre environs, leaving his Alana to the crushing coils of that loathsome serpent in the cave.

"Die pig!" Xusia exclaimed, turning on his death-wish for Talon full force.

A pathetic, muffled cry from Alana in the cave turned Xusia's head for a moment—but just long enough for Talon to raise his tri-bladed sword and fire the middle, spring-loaded blade.

The flashing missile ripped through the flesh and meat of Xusia's right shoulder, taking him utterly unaware. He staggered and whirled around in pain. "Vile boy!" he hissed and then crashed to the ground, alive but gushing blood from a massive wound in the shoulder.

With the collapse of Xusia the force that pinned both Talon and Cromwell to the stone floor snapped, and they both rushed to their feet, anxious to finish the death-duel they had started earlier. Though still wobbly and dazed from Xusia's pummeling magic, they approached each other with renewed appetite for one another's blood. Cromwell pointed to Talon's tri-bladed sword. "Of course you've got the advantage. I've one blade—you've three."

Talon fired the second spring-loaded blade onto the floor of the chamber, where it skittered clangorously along the wet stones.

"There. Does that make you happy, outlaw king?"

207

Cromwell sneered, taking his first fierce whack at Talon, missing his ear by inches. "I shall never be happy until I run my sword through your pretty face, sir!"

Their swords relentlessly bit, hammered, thrust, swung and sliced at each other, causing a continuous dazzle of bright metal in the shadowy chamber. Every lethal trick, technique and stratagem at their disposal was played out, but still neither grunting and cursing swordsman could best the other.

Then Talon remembered the serpent with his pretty catch in the cave. "My God—Alana!" He tried to sidestep Cromwell and raced for the cave. But the agile king jumped in front of him, hoping to capitalize on Talon's distraction.

"Out of my way!" Talon roared again, slicing wildly at Cromwell's head, but the king blocked the assault.

"Help!" came the choked cry from the cave.

Alana's plight triggered a renewed flurry of flying sword cuts from Talon, and they were so swift and constant that Cromwell felt he was beset by a hundred swooshing and flashing blades instead of just one. Talon's love's sweet life was in danger and he had no time to dally or engage in the subtleties of swordsmanship. He brought this now decidedly one-sided contest to a swift and deadly finish by dropping to his knees when the king's sword swirled over his head and rammed his own blade straight through Cromwell's middle. "Ugh!" the king grunted, doubling over and toppling to the ground on his back. A fountain of blood spurted from the ugly gash in his stomach. His royal white and gold wedding vestments were quickly soaked in blood.

Talon leaped over the king's convulsing body and bounded toward the cave.

"A last request," Cromwell gasped. "Who are you?"

"Talon, son of the good king you murdered!" he shouted over his shoulder, never looking back.

"I almost forgot about you." His voice was fading.

"Never have I forgotten about you!" he rejoindered to a dead man.

Just before Talon crossed the threshold of the cave he retrieved the second blade from his sword off the ground. With the blade remounted, he plunged into the dark belly of the cave, never having noticed that Xusia was nowhere in sight.

The luminously white serpent was long enough to be a dragon. Fortunately as Talon crept up on the snake he saw that it was more interested in toying with its soft, pretty catch than eating or crushing it. And every time Alana whimpered—and whimpers were all that the snake's arresting coils allowed her to make—the soft baby cries of hurt would make the serpent stir a little, as if the sounds gave it pleasure. The reptile's velvety movements were in slow-motion time—like Death lazily debating taking or not taking a life. It kept ponderously winding around Alana's limp form as if it had all of eternity to play with this pink, soft toy.

It was the crunching of dirt under Talon's boots that brought the mammoth worm into electric alertness. The snake's convex head shot up and swiveled around to track the noise with such quickness and readiness to strike that a second's delay would surely have cost Alana and Talon their lives.

Before the serpent had time to stick its forked tongue out twice, a single blade from Talon's firing sword severed its huge head, causing the coils that held Alana to collapse like a long string suddenly untied.

With the mammoth reptile stretched its full length dead at their feet, Talon bent to clasp Alana's outstretched hand, her face now radiant with relief and love. But before she could take his hand, a movement in a dark niche behind Talon caught her eye and she cried out, "Behind you, Talon!"

Talon instinctively ducked and spun around—sword in hand—only to incredulously find himself confronting Xusia, wounded but about to bring a stone ax down on his head. Talon dodged the blow and plunged the remaining blade of his weapon into the sorcerer's chest, opening up another fountain of blood.

"Damn you through eternity!" Xusia howled, while Talon stabbed his collapsing body again and again.

As much as she despised the fiend, Alana had to hide her eyes from Talon's merciless, gory thrusts and slices.

The sorcerer impaled on the end of his blade like a long eel in robes, Talon hoisted Xusia over his head and dashed him on the cave's rocky floor. Still the sorcerer's gashed and broken body billowed with angry life. It wasn't until Talon grabbed the hilt of the sword with both hands and plunged the blade straight through the wizard's heart that Xusia stopped breathing.

As stout of heart as Talon was, he too had to look away from the horribly mutilated body of

210

Xusia, for it looked as if a pack of wolves had torn it apart.

Talon now helped Alana to her feet and pulled her away from the gory sight of the dead snake and the sundered sorcerer. At the lip of the cave, where there was enough torchlight for them to gaze into each other's faces, Talon took Alana into his strong arms and they had their first kiss. Their bodies longed for each other and while she trembled he tensed.

Alana pulled her tongue out of his mouth to look deep into his diamond-blue eyes. "Talon! Dear, precious Talon! Is it really you? Childhood hero of my dreams!"

"Yes, my darling! The same Talon who used to pull your hair and then, later, had dewy fantasies about you while watching the rabbits and horses make love!"

She blushed and wrinkled her nose at him. He couldn't resist crushing her mouth with his once more. After they kissed so long that she had to unglue her lips from his to catch her breath, Alana was amused to see that Talon was ready for more than just romantic kisses.

She brushed her lips against his bare chest and stepped back. "Easy, my love. We should get back to my brother. He must be worried sick about us."

Alana started ahead of him but Talon reached for her hand and made her stop for a moment. "I hope you haven't forgotten our bargain, Alana?" he asked, husky of voice.

She smiled. "I always keep my word, Talon," she replied, melting all over, it seemed. "But must it be here—in these awful surroundings?"

Talon resignedly sighed. "I've waited all these

years for you, my darling, I suppose I can wait another hour or two."

Before she realized what he was about, Talon swept her off her feet into his arms and began to walk with her out of the catacombs. "I know a soft, green, woodsy hill high above Elysium—the perfect place for sowing the seeds of eternal love. What say you, my sweet lady?"

"I've always loved planting things and watching them grow!"

Dawn bathed the courtyard with pink light, bringing into bold relief the spoils of last night's siege. In the midst of the upturned tables, broken wine casks and piles of dumped food was strewn the grim litter of chopped noblemen and Klaws. Only a short time ago the serfs and servants of the castle had started carrying out the corpses from the courtyard to a site beyond the moat for a massive funeral pyre.

Although the battle was an unqualified victory for the rebellion, a pall of grave concern hung over the battle-weary men who won it, their dress stained with gore, while they sipped wine, chatted idly with the slave girls or slept to replenish their sapped strength. For the triumph was hollow without the man who, more than any single warrior, had been responsible for winning it. Any thought of a victory celebration was out of the question until Talon and the fair Alana—whom he had set out to retrieve from Cromwell and Machelli—were safely among them once again.

If Talon and Alana were not restored to them soon that could only signify that the king had instrumented some kind of ill fate for them. Furthermore, if Cromwell still lived that augured he would soon return with the full force of his armies guarding the borders. If that were the case, the contender for the throne, Mikah, would find himself trying to hold the castle with a skeletal crew of fighters; the citizens of Elysium, fearing Cromwell's retaliation, would never rally around Mikah as the legitimate heir to the throne until they saw the king's crown on his own head.

While Darius, Morgan and Rodrigo conversed with the concubines, the six kings who had risked their lives for Talon were sitting around a table lugubriously discussing these weighty matters with Mikah, when the clatter of approaching hooves instantly pricked their ears. An untrammeled silence immediately prevailed throughout the courtyard, as the sound of a galloping charger grew closer and closer.

"Could it be him?" Mikah whispered, articulating everyone's thoughts at the table, his clean-cut features suffused with straining hope.

The air in the courtyard seemed to crackle with expectation and unspoken excitement, as the mount and its unknown rider galloped nearer and nearer to the main entrance. Slowly the throng of mercenaries, pirates, kings, slave girls, concubines and servants rose to their feet, gazing longingly at the courtyard entrance.

When the crowd heard the pound of the horse's hooves crossing the drawbridge the tension reached a peak of anticipation that was almost unendurable in its intensity.

Suddenly the man who had been uppermost in their minds for hours—a hero's hero and beloved watchdog of fair play—came charging into the courtyard astride a raging black stallion, Alana clinging to his waist behind him. The happy sight of the wild-eyed, brave and bloodied warrior was so riveting that the crowd's enthusiasm hung suspended in awed silence for another moment.

Talon reared his horse high in triumph and yelled to the wide-eyed mob of fighters and friends.

"Ho, all you rogues, rascals and wenches! Why the long faces? Did you think the ogre Cromwell got me, perchance? Well, I bring you glad tidings! The outlaw king is dead! Rejoice, brothers and sisters! You've snatched a kingdom back from a thief!"

And now the tidal wave of excitement that had been dammed back broke, flooding the courtyard with tumultuous roars of unbridled jubilation. In an explosive flash the night's worries and tensions were washed away, leaving clean, joyous spirits that were but minutes ago leaden prophets of doom. The cheering, shouting and jumping crowd clamored and eddied around the two panting riders as if they wanted to lift Talon and Alana from the horse onto their shoulders. But Talon discouraged any such action with a wave of his hand. Then he spotted Mikah nearby but having trouble cutting through the tight press to him and Alana. Talon brought Cromwell's bejeweled crown into view. At the sight of the crown another wave of jubilation swept through the crowd. Talon tossed the glittering crown to Mikah's outstretched hand.

"Wear it in good health, your majesty!"

Mikah's face was a sunburst of smiles. He placed the crown on his handsome head. The cries of joy that went up from the crowd was deafening. The men nearest to the new king hoisted Mikah onto their shoulders, Talon and Alana watching with moist eyes. Raised above his adoring subjects, Mikah motioned that the crowd hoist his childhood friend and beloved sister to their shoulders too.

But Talon averted the rush toward him again by rearing his steed once more and spurring it towards the entrance through which they came. An ecstatic dual chant now spread throughout the courtyard: "Long live the king! Talon! Long live the king! Talon!"

But Talon would not be deterred. As much as he enjoyed basking in the glory, he enjoyed the prospect of being alone with Alana on the hill even more. As he began to trot out of the courtyard—Alana clinging to him with even bolder embrace—Talon waved goodbye to Mikah. When he saw the six kings standing on the table shouting "Talon! Talon!" with the commoners, he smiled at the miracle of equality the victory had wrought and waved at them too, shouting, "I hope your majesties will have further need of my services! For I will soon have a wife to support!"

This announcement caused the mob to surge toward Talon and Alana with even greater excitement but Talon continued to spur his horse onward to the archway.

"Take us with you!" Darius pleaded with his leader, running beside Talon's powerful charger. Talon winked at his friend and reached around to pat the outside of Alana's thigh.

"This is one venture I share with no man, Darius!"

* * *

By noon, bodies stickily entangled atop a soft green carpet of grass, under a shaded canopy of leafy branches, Talon delivered Alana from the burden of her maidenhead.

At that luminous moment in their lives neither of the happily sated pair had cause to be anything but blissfully hopeful about their immediate future. They had been reunited and they loved each other implicitly, body, mind, and soul. Mikah was king. Cromwell was dead. And the abominable sorcerer was no longer free to roam through Eh-Dan wreaking havoc as his malevolent spirit so inclined.

Thus it appeared. But sometimes the gods provide man with an idyllic holiday before unleashing a raging pack of dogs upon his serenity. At least that is the way it looked for these two lovers. For at the precise moment that Talon and Alana transcended themselves in a union of ineffable bliss—a blaze of ecstasy that seemed to carry them to the stars and moon and back—another kind of bliss was being experienced in a secret cove a dozen miles west of Elysium's harbor.

A small, black galleon, with no visible sailors raising its anchor or hoisting its sails, was slowly plying its way out to sea, operating with the smoothness of a full crew.

The only sign of life was a life that defied comprehension, logic and any human compassion (for how can pure evil inspire compassion?). It was a form of life that appeared to be the outgrowth of a grotesque union between the human, demonic and reptilian worlds. And the bliss that this hybrid creature experienced while standing at the stern of the galleon—a thousand sword cuts in its body slowly and mysteriously closing without scars—was the bliss of merciless revenge he plotted, gazing back at the Kingdom of Eh-Dan he was leaving—but only long enough for Xusia to recharge his powers.